the difference

NEW YORK TIMES BESTSELLING AUTHOR
KAYLEE RYAN

Cover Design: Sommer Stein, Perfect Pear Creative Covers
Cover Photography: Sara Eirew
Models: Simon Cooki & Pamlea Tremblay Mcallen
Editing: Hot Tree Editing
Formatting: Integrity Formatting
Proofreading: Deaton Author Services

chapter
one

Addyson

"What about that one?" My best friend, Harper, points her finger over my shoulder. I don't need to look to know that I'm not interested. I do it anyway to appease her.

"Which one?" I turn to look over my shoulder at the group of guys playing darts.

"The one with the black tank top."

"Negative." We're sitting at Stagger, a local bar, having drinks for our weekly girls' night. "I told you, Harp. I'm swearing off men. I'm over the drama."

"Oh, come on. You can't let a few bad dates and relationships take you out of the game."

"That's exactly what I'm doing. I'm tired of the games. I want something normal, and from my history, that's not possible, so I'm sitting the bench." I'm not exaggerating. Bad luck should have been my middle name when it comes to the opposite sex. I'm not saying I'm benched forever, but I'm definitely on the injured reserve for the foreseeable future.

"It's not that bad." This time she says and points her cheese stick at me before taking a bite.

"Right," I say dramatically. "What about Anthony?"

"Pfft, he was a dick. He cheated on you. That doesn't mean you fail at relationships."

"I didn't say that I failed. I said I have bad luck. Okay, what about Tommy?"

She shrugs. "You can't help that he was batting for the other team."

"Harper, he was using me as a cover. Do you know how humiliating that is? To think you are in a committed, loving relationship to find out your man likes men?" I really liked Tommy. In fact, we still keep in touch. Just random "how are you" messages. He and his boyfriend, Josh, are happy and finally have the acceptance of Tommy's parents. I guess when they figured out how far he was willing to go to make them happy, they changed their way of thinking.

"He cared about you."

"That's not the point," I argue. I know he cared about me, but he also deceived me. That's a hard pill to swallow.

"Still not an excuse to take yourself out of the game," she counters.

"Okay, fine. What about Jared?" I raise an eyebrow in question.

"He was a douche."

I smirk. "You think? He was so hot for you. I should have caught on since he was always asking if you were going to be there when we went out." Hindsight and all that. I thought it was great the new guy in my life was supportive of how close Harper and I are. We've been friends since preschool and share an unbreakable bond.

"He got what was coming to him." She grins.

"That he did." I can't help but smile as I raise my glass to hers, and we tap them together. Jared and I dated for about two months. It ended the night he cornered Harper at the club we were at. He told her he was only with me to get to know her, that he loved her. She kneed him in the balls, bringing him to his knees. She left him there to come and find me. I haven't seen or heard from him since.

"You can't let any of those encounters keep you from moving forward." She signals to the waitress and holds up two fingers and her empty glass.

"Really? Shall we talk about Fletcher?"

She immediately laughs, covering her mouth with her hand to keep from spewing the drink of beer she just took all over me. "I'm sorry," she says, removing her hand. "I'm not laughing at you, but with you."

"You think it's funny that I spent three months with a man who couldn't get me off?" I ask incredulously. Fletcher was my last adventure with dating, and that was over six months ago. Harper has been on me to get back out there. I have no desire. Well, I have desire, but that's nothing that I can't handle on my own. Sure, I'd like to feel the strength of a man hovering over me, holding me after, but sacrifices and all that. In my present state of thinking, it's well worth it.

"It's not that. It's the way you would tell the story. You tried to coach him and everything." She giggles.

She's not wrong. I tried giving him pointers, but nothing seemed to help. To top it off, he was surprised when I ended things between us. He was convinced I was the one. I'm not sure why he thinks that any woman is okay with him getting his and not repaying the favor. Like I said, I'm better off handling things on my own. This is what my life has become. Sitting at a bar with my best friend while she giggles like a teenager over my lack of orgasms.

Just living my best life.

"I'm telling you. I had to break it off for fear of getting carpal tunnel." I hold up my right hand and wiggle my wrist around, and she laughs even harder.

I fail to find the humor.

"One discrete online order and that little problem was taken care of." I smile, proud of myself for taking charge of the situation.

"Sounds like you need a real man," a deep, husky voice whispers in my ear, causing tingles to race up and down my spine.

Rotating in my seat, I take him in. Tall, well over six feet, dark hair, well-trimmed beard, and a sleeve of ink. Add in the deep, husky timbre of his voice, and you have sex on legs. For a fraction of a second, I reconsider my "sitting the bench" plan, but shake out of the thought quickly.

"Thanks, but I spend my time with the battery-operated variety these days," I say, turning back in my seat.

"Mind if we join you?" he asks.

Harper gives me a wide-eyed "you better scoot your ass over and make room" look, so that's what I do. Spinning to face the sexy stranger, I offer him my hand. "Addyson Stafford."

His large hand engulfs mine. "Lucas Prescott."

I'm tongue-tied. He's gorgeous and exudes confidence. "Addy." Harper breaks me out of my trance, and I realize I've been staring at him. I turn to look at her, and she motions toward the guy next to her. He's equally as good-looking, maybe a little less rugged than my guy. No, not my guy. Just the dark-haired handsome stranger who seems to be talking to me more so than Harper. "Addyson," I say, holding my hand out for him across the table.

"Justin Atwood. Nice to meet you, ladies," he says, turning

his gaze back to Harper. I must have missed their introduction while I was drooling over Lucas.

"So, orgasms." Lucas smirks, taking a drink from the bottle of beer in his hand that I'm just now noticing.

"Ugh." I cover my face with my hands. "We do not need to rehash that conversation."

"Oh, no, I really think we should." I can hear the grin in his voice.

"Addy has had a bad run lately," Harper chimes in.

"Bad run? Really?" I question her. "Bad run is ending a long-term relationship. I'm having more than a bad run."

"A few hiccups." She tries to soothe my ruffled feathers.

"Okay, let's continue with the list," I say, not even caring that one of the sexiest guys I've ever laid eyes on is sitting right next to me, his thigh pressed against mine. "What about Blake?"

She cringes. "Asshole."

"What happened?" Justin asks. He sits back in the booth, settling in for the story.

"Oh, you know, we met at the coffee shop my senior year of college. We exchanged numbers; he called the next day." I take a drink of my beer before continuing. "We went out a few times, and he suggested he cook me dinner. Finals were coming up and were kicking my ass. I readily agreed. He picked me up from class as I rode with Harper that day. We stopped at the store to get everything he needed and guess who we ran into?" I keep my gaze on Justin though I'm unable to forget the man sitting next to me. "His wife," I say when he shrugs. "We met her in the produce aisle. Have you ever had a cucumber thrown at your head? Not pleasant." I shake off my irritation. "I could go on and on." I take another sip of beer.

"Is he the same schmuck who couldn't get you there?" Lucas asks.

I turn to look at him. "Nope, that was Fletcher."

"Just how many are there?" he questions.

"Enough." I shrug. "They've all been disasters waiting to happen. Hence the reason I'm on the bench."

"Every benched player needs practice." He winks.

"You doubting my skills, Prescott?" I lean into him.

"No doubts," he says huskily. "But if you need someone to… throw a few balls with, I'm your guy."

"Do you even like baseball?" Harper laughs.

"Nope." I shrug, finishing off my beer. All three of them are laughing, and it takes extreme effort to fight my grin.

I'm making light of it, but in all honesty, I'm just over it all. The effort you put into dating and relationships to get nothing in return. Don't get me wrong, I'm not a diva, but an orgasm or two might be nice. Oh, and to be the only one in your life, for that person to be into you and not your best friend, or be into someone of the same gender. Is that too much to ask?

"All right, so give me some more," Lucas says, bumping his shoulder into mine. He's flirting and I must admit, the contact is welcome. With my self-imposed drought, this is the only contact I'm going to be seeing for a while.

"I'm sure you have better things to do than listen to me whine about my dating mishaps."

"Got a cold beer." He shows me his new bottle that was just dropped off at our table, along with two more drafts for Harper and me. "I'm all ears."

"Fine," I grumble. "Let's see." I take a drink as I sift through my bad experiences to give him another one. "Oh." I point to Harper. "What about Rodney?"

She shakes her head. "That one was scary."

"Scary?" Lucas sits up a little straighter.

"Yeah, so I signed up for online dating. Thinking maybe I just wasn't going to the right places to meet a decent guy. Rodney was an immediate match. We talked back and forth online for a couple of months before I was brave enough to meet him."

"Did you meet this guy alone?" he asks. Concern is evident in his voice. The knowledge warms me. This man doesn't know me, but he's concerned about me. His shoulders are tense, so I'm quick to diffuse his worry.

"No, we met at a bar a town over and Harper was with me, but sitting at the bar."

"Like that's protection," he grumbles, but I ignore him and continue with the story.

"So, on his online profile, he was a decent-looking guy, blond hair, green eyes, said he was a runner. He had an athletic build in the picture, so it was believable." I take another drink, feeling a little vulnerable with the attention of both of these gorgeous guys. Maybe telling these stories isn't such a good idea.

"What happened?" Justin asks.

Too far in to turn back now. "We finally agreed to meet for drinks. I got there early so Harper could settle in at the bar, just in case. So I'm sitting at the booth waiting for him. I keep watching the door looking for him. I had his profile pulled up on my phone and everything." I take another drink. "When an older gentleman, late fifties if I had to guess, slides into the booth and hands me a white rose."

"Was it him?"

"Yep," I say, popping the *p.* "When I called him out on it, he said he wanted me to want him for him. I then had to point out that he lied not only about his looks, but his age, and occupation and I'm sure everything else. When I stood to leave, he grabbed my hand, telling me one night with him and he'd make it worth my while."

"That's where I stepped in," Harper adds. "I was sitting next to a couple of guys, leather vests, scruffy beards. We later learned they were in a motorcycle club. Anyway, when I saw him grab her, I enlisted the two guys to show him to the door."

"You learned your lesson, right? No more meeting up with

strange men from the internet," Lucas says.

"Well, you should probably go. You are a stranger," I tell him. The words leave my lips but oddly enough, I almost want him to stay. He seems like a nice guy, but then again, history proves my judgment in men is shit. Still, a girl can wish.

"But I'm sitting right here. You see me. What you see is what you get." He winks again, and butterflies take flight in my belly. He really is that gorgeous.

"Yeah, but that doesn't mean I should trust you," I counter.

"I guess only time will tell." He raises his hand to grab the waitress's attention and orders us all another round.

That's how the night goes. The four of us sit and talk, leisurely drinking a few beers, and I have to say, even with the intrusion on girls' night it's welcome.

"Last call," the waitress says, stopping by our table.

"You ladies want another?" Justin asks.

"No, thanks," Harper and I say at the same time.

"You ready?" I look across the booth at my friend. I can tell she's really interested in Justin. If I were not on a dating freeze, I would be crushing on Lucas as well, but I've been down that road. It's one I'm not ready to travel again anytime soon.

"Yes." She turns to Justin. "It was nice meeting you," she tells him. I miss his reply because Lucas's hot breath is in my ear.

"I had a good time." His deep timbre causes goose bumps to break out across my skin.

"Me too." I smile over at him. His lips look soft.

"Can I borrow your phone?" he asks.

"Sure." I dig into my bag, unlock the screen, and hand it to him. I watch as his fingers fly across the screen. "What exactly are you doing?" I assume he needed to call an Uber or a friend to pick them up.

"Sending myself a text."

"Why?" I ask stupidly. I know the answer to that question. I cringe inwardly. You would think this is the first time I've been in the presence of a man.

"So, we can do this again." He nods across the table. "My boy has no game." He chuckles. "This way when he's kicking himself in the ass tomorrow for not doing what I just did, I can help him out."

"Why not ask me for her number?" I ask him.

"What would be the fun in that?"

"Right, well, if he wants her number, you know how to find me," I say, taking my phone out of his hands and dropping it back in my bag.

"How are you getting home?" he asks.

"Oh, I just live a few blocks away. We walked."

"It's late."

"Is it?" I reply sassily.

"We'll walk you."

"That's not necessary. We're big girls. How are you getting home?" I ask, turning the tables on him.

"I called my sister. Ollie, my nephew is staying with our parents tonight. I tried to get her to come out with us, but she was actually looking forward to a quiet night at home. She insisted we call her, and she would come and get us. I didn't bother to argue. If Anna is anything, she's determined to get her way."

I can't help but wonder if sister is code for girlfriend or wife. Like I said, I'm jaded.

"You don't want to keep her waiting."

"If you were my sister, I would want the guy to make sure she got home safe."

"So, you trying to find out where I live? What, you want to stalk me now?"

"No." He rubs his temples. "I just want to make sure that the two of you get home safe."

"Hey, did you call Anna yet?" Justin asks Lucas. "I think we should walk them home."

Lucas looks over at me and smirks. "Yes, but I told her to wait about fifteen minutes before she heads this way. I was thinking the same thing."

"We're fine," I protest.

"It's not that far," Harper says half-heartedly. I can tell she's not ready to say goodbye.

"It's settled then." Justin slides out of the booth and offers her his hand. Lucas does the same, and I'm on to his game, but I let him help me out of the booth all the same. No point in causing a scene and ruining Harper's night.

The night air is sticky, but the sky is clear, as clear as it can be in the city. Justin and Harper walk ahead of us, walking close, their arms touching, hands open as if one is waiting for the other to take charge.

"He's a good guy," Lucas says.

"Yeah? What about you?"

He laughs. "You can trust us."

"You'll have to excuse me if I don't buy that line. Did you already forget my dating history woes?"

"So, you want to date me?" he asks, grinning.

"You know what I mean." I smack at his arm playfully, and his grin grows even wider.

"I do." He pulls out his phone. His fingers tap away at the screen before he puts it back in his pocket. "I sent you a message."

Sure enough, my phone beeps. Pulling it out of my bag, I see a new message from Lucas Prescott. Clicking on it, I see his full name and an address. Followed by a picture.

"You keep a picture of your license on your phone?" I ask him.

"I had to send it to my insurance agent for my car insurance renewal. He was traveling while I called him. He told me to text it to him, so I sent him a pic of my license. That prevents me from transposing the numbers, and it was faster." He shakes his head. "You have my info. So rest assured that you're safe with me knowing where you live."

"So you keep trying to convince me."

"You're a hard nut to crack, Addyson."

I shrug. "Yeah, I didn't used to be. Life has hardened me. You seem like a great guy, Lucas, but it's going to take more than a few beers and a chivalrous walk home to convince me that you're worth trusting. I no longer give that freely." I can't risk another gash in my heart. I've been down that road too many times to count. It's more than just a broken heart. I've been used, lied to, cheated on. The list is endless. I need a break from the drama dating brings to my life.

"Sounds like a challenge to me. I guess I'll just have to prove it to you."

I have to make an effort to not roll my eyes. He talks a good game but so did all of the others. "You do that," I say, not really caring what he thinks he has to prove. Same old song and dance.

"This is me," I say when we reach Harper and Justin. They're sitting on the front step of my condo.

"Roommates?" Lucas asks.

"No, best friends since we were like three." I laugh.

"Those are rare these days."

"Don't I know it."

"Well, ladies." Justin stands. "It was a pleasure. We should do this again sometime." He never takes his eyes off Harper.

"Definitely." She grins up at him.

"Catch you later." Lucas lightly leans his shoulder into mine before they turn and head back to the bar. I watch as he lifts his phone to his ear, calling his sister, or who he claims to be his sister to let her know they're on their way back to the bar.

"Addy," Harper squeals. "Best girls' night ever."

"It was a good night," I agree, walking up the steps and unlocking my condo door. We sit on the couch for a while, and she talks about how much she likes Justin, and how great of a guy they both seem to be. I have to agree with her as far as first impressions go, they gave a good one. The true test will be if they reach out to us.

"Did you give him your number?" I ask.

"No." She sighs dramatically and leans her head back against the couch. "I ruined it."

"I gave Lucas mine, well, kind of. He asked to use my phone and texted himself."

"Wow, what happened to sitting the bench?"

"Him stealing my number has nothing to do with me and the bench. He claimed that Justin would forget to ask for yours, claiming his friend has no game, and he wanted to be able to give it to him."

"Did he take my number too?"

"No."

Her eyes crinkle with mischief. "I see." She grins.

"You see nothing. I'm going to bed. Show yourself to your room." I stand, and head down the hall. My spare room is set up for her and hers for me. We contemplated living together, but we wanted our own space. Nothing says adulting like paying rent on your own space all alone.

Climbing into bed, I can't help but replay the night. I'm happy for Harper. She needs a good man in her life. She's not had the dating woes that I have, but then again, her walls were taller than mine. Not anymore. My walls are constructed and it's going to take one hell of an army, or one hell of a man, to bring them down.

chapter
two

LUCAS

My ass barely hits the chair Monday morning before Justin is striding into my office.

"I messed up," he says, plopping down in the seat across from my desk.

"Tell me more." I struggle to contain my amusement.

"I didn't get her number. Who does that?" He throws his hands in the air in frustration. "I mean, we talked all night, walked them home, and my dumb ass failed to get her number. I spent all day yesterday trying to look her up online. She could be the one, and I fucked it all up," he sighs and relaxes against the seat.

"You done?" A grin tilts my lips.

He glares at me. "Why in the hell are you smiling? Wait." He studies me. "Please tell me you got Addyson's number?" He's bright-eyed and eager.

"Maybe."

He scoots to the edge of his seat, pulling his phone out of his pocket, tapping the screen before looking up at me. "Let me have it."

"Not so fast. First of all, I don't have Harper's number, and second, you can't call right now."

"Why the hell not?"

"We need a plan."

"We?"

"Yes, we."

"And me calling Harper, the one woman I've met in recent months who is laidback and doesn't seem to understand that I'm an Atwood is not a good enough plan?"

"No. You like this girl. You can't just call and say hey, do you like me? Check yes or no. You must have a plan. Dinner? Movie? Something. You have to call with a plan. Let her know you've been thinking about her and can't wait to see her again. You reveal the plan, letting her know you really have thought about it."

"Right. Yeah, good idea." He laughs. "Now what's mine?"

"How old are you again?"

"Twenty-nine, and this is a first for me. I've never had to try. I tell them my last name and all bets are off. Hell, half of the time they already know who I am."

Justin Atwood is loaded. Well, his family is loaded and him by association. His grandfather was involved in the food service industry, making enough money that Justin's grandkids never have to work a day in their lives. Justin has a trust fund that he's never touched, choosing to make his own way in the world. He's a damn fine architect. We went to college together where he graduated a year before me. When it was time for my externship, he gave me the inside track here at our firm. Like him, they offered me a job as soon as it was over.

"Exactly," I tell him. "It's why you need to have your shit in order before you call. Besides, I don't have Harper's number. I have Addyson's, remember?"

"You interested?" he asks me.

"You heard her, right? She's jaded. And in no way is looking."

"Not what I asked you," he says, calling me out.

"She's gorgeous, but she's not into it."

"Why'd you take her number?"

"One, I knew you would forget. I could tell you were really into Harper, and that's not something I've seen with you before. Two, she's a good time, and it never hurts to have the number of a beautiful woman."

"I need something… epic."

"Epic?" I raise my eyebrows.

"First date and all that." He shrugs.

"Right, so what you got?"

"Dinner?"

"You call dinner epic?" I counter.

"Fine, what do you suggest?"

"I'll ask Addyson." I grab my phone and fire off a text.

Me:	Hey, so Justin's crazy about your girl.
Addyson:	Is that so?
Me:	Yep. He wants to ask her out but wants it to be "epic."
Addyson:	Epic, huh? What's he thinking?
Me:	That's where you come in.

"What's she saying?" Justin asks.

"Nothing yet. I told her you wanted the date to be epic."

He groans. "Kill me now." I throw my head back in laughter.

| Addyson: | We have plans this weekend and she works Friday |

night.

Me: Care to let me in on those plans?

Addyson: I don't know…

Me: Come on, Addyson. We're the good guys.

Addyson: That is yet to be determined.

Addyson: But she likes him too.

Addyson: There's a festival going on at St. Pierre Park on Saturday. We go every year.

Me: We'll see you there.

Addyson: Tell Justin he better not make me regret this.

Me: She's in good hands.

I wait for her reply, but it never comes. Tossing my phone back on my desk, I look at Justin. He's still sitting on the edge of his seat, watching me, waiting for me to tell him. "I guess there's a festival this weekend at St. Pierre Park. Addyson says she and Harper go every year. Harper has to work Friday night, so this is your only shot this weekend."

"We could go to dinner one night this week."

"You could," I agree. "Or you and I can go to this festival and we can run into them. Then you can ask for her number on your own."

Slowly, he nods. "Yeah, that could work. Did she say anything?"

"Focus. We are not in junior high." I chuckle. "She said Harper was into you, and to not make her regret telling us where they'll be."

"That's it?"

"That's it."

"Looks like we're going to a festival." He stands and straightens his tie.

"What if I had plans this weekend?"

"Cancel them."

My laughter follows him out of my office door. Grabbing my phone, I fire off another text.

Me: We're in. What time?

Addyson: Six.

Me: Where?

Addyson: Come on now, where's the fun in that? I told you where we would be. It's up to you to find us.

I smile down at my phone.

Me: See you Saturday.

This time I don't wait for the reply that I know won't come. Instead, I call Justin.

"I just left your office," he says in greeting.

"They're going to be there Saturday at six."

"Right."

"So we need to be there at least at five thirty."

"Why?"

"Because we're not meeting them there. We have to find them."

"Done."

"You're driving."

He laughs. "I don't care who drives as long as I get to see her again and this time get her damn number."

"What would you do without me?"

His reply is laughter and the line going dead. Pushing our weekend plans from my mind, I get busy on the plans that I have spread out on the table in my office. Time to earn my paycheck. Lucky for me I have a job that I love.

chapter
three

Addyson

I haven't told Harper that Lucas and Justin might be at the festival today. I didn't want to get her hopes up. I've been down that road too many times to count, and if I can spare that for my best friend, I will. Besides, even if they do show up, who says they'll actually find us. I probably should have told him that we would meet them, but where's the fun in that? Justin needs to work for it if he wants her. Harper deserves that and nothing less.

Even though I have no intentions of dating, I still take my time getting ready. Just because I'm not interested doesn't mean I don't want to impress. Besides, a night of flirting with Lucas doesn't sound so terrible. With one final glance in the mirror, I grab my phone and crossbody purse. Making sure I have my keys, I head out the door. I told Harper I'd drive today. Just in case there is an off chance that they do show up, and they hit it off, I wanted to give her an easy out for him to drive her home. I'm not a complete hater when it comes to relationships and men, just when it involves me. I'm cursed in some way.

When I pull into Harper's apartment complex, she's sitting outside on the bench, nose buried in her phone. I blow the horn, causing her to jump. I laugh when she scrambles to keep from dropping her phone.

"Nice welcome." She smiles as she buckles herself into the passenger seat.

"Hey, I do what I can," I tease.

"I'm starving. I swear my mouth is watering just thinking about the festival food."

"You and me both. That's the only reason I go."

"Come on, you love the atmosphere as much as I do."

"You're not wrong. There's just something about it that brings back childhood memories, but I wouldn't be destroyed emotionally if I never got to go again. I mean, if they were no longer serving food."

She throws her head back against the seat and howls with laughter. "You and me both. All I've had today is a banana. I needed to save room." She pats her flat stomach. "So, have you talked to Lucas?"

I've been waiting for this question to pop up. "Yeah, he texted me earlier in the week."

"What? When? Why didn't you tell me?" She fires off questions.

"This," I say, taking a hand off the wheel and pointing at her, "is why. I knew you would freak out."

"I'm not freaking out," she backtracks. "I just don't know why you didn't tell me."

Here goes nothing. "Because I wanted it to be a surprise."

"What?"

I quickly glance over at her, before putting my eyes back on the road. Her brow is furrowed; she's utterly confused. "They're coming today. Well, I think they are. Lucas said they'd be here."

She reaches over and smacks my arm. "And you didn't tell me. Look at me." She looks down at her cut-off jean shorts and flip-flops. "I'm a mess."

"No, you're you, Harper. That's why I didn't tell you. I know how much you like this guy after only a few hours at the bar. I wanted you to be you. If he can't like you for who you are, then you don't need him in your life."

"But I could have made an effort."

I laugh. "You did. Your hair is curled, you have on makeup, and your cut-offs show off your legs. You look like you, beautiful as always."

"What time are they coming? Are we meeting them?"

This part is probably going to piss her off. "Well," I say slowly. "I told them what time we would be here, and they're going to find us."

"What do you mean? They're going to find us?"

"I didn't exactly make plans with them. I told them where we would be and what time. I told him that if they found us, we could all hang out."

"Why? Why would you do that?"

"He needs to work for it."

"He's not one of your laundry list of guys who's shit on you, Addy. He's a great guy who I believe actually liked talking to me and didn't even try to get me back to his place or in the back of his car." She stops talking, and I wait her out. I've known her long enough to know she's not done yet. "This isn't even about me, is it? This is about you. About you and Lucas."

"What?" It's my turn to be surprised. "No. I mean, yes, he's hot as hell, but I told you. I'm on a break. A really nice, long break."

"Then why not give him my number to give to Justin? Why

the game?"

"I want to see you happy. If he finds you here, you'll know he's really into you. He's not looking for easy. He's willing to put in the work."

"It's a festival, Addyson."

"Right, but there are going to be thousands of people there. It's like finding a needle in a haystack."

"Exactly!" she says, exasperated. "They might never find us."

"True, but what if they do?" I ask, pulling into a prime parking spot and turning off the engine. I feel a twinge of guilt. I know she likes him and wants to get to know him. I probably should have just told them where to meet us. However, I like the idea of him working for her affection. He needs to earn it. It's better to find out now if he's not willing to put in the effort.

"Two hours." She holds up two fingers. "If they have not found us in two hours, we're calling Lucas, and we're going to tell them where we are."

"Fine," I concede. I have a feeling they're going to find us. Neither one of them appear to be men who back down from a challenge. Lucas, I'm sure will be on the lookout for the simple fact that I insinuated he needed to find us.

"What are we eating first?" she asks as we step up to the gate.

I'm relieved she seems to have forgiven me. "I'll leave that up to you," I concede.

"Definitely getting a lemonade," she says, pointing to the first food booth we see. We're standing in line when I feel hot breath against my ear.

"Found you." His deep timbre causes chills to race up my spine.

Turning to look over my shoulder, I see Lucas smiling at me, his face still close. So close I could lean in and kiss him. "How long have you been here?" I ask him.

"Not long."

I look over to see Justin and Harper already deep in conversation. He has his phone out, and my guess is he's getting her number. "You could have sent him on his own," I tell Lucas.

He steps back, but I can still smell him all around me. "And let you be the third wheel all by your lonesome? What kind of guy would I be if I did that? Besides, everyone loves a good festival, and on the off chance we didn't find you…." He shrugs.

"Are you trying to tell me you have a nice guy in that bad-boy exterior, Lucas Prescott?"

"Depends." His voice dips low.

"Yeah? On what?" I ask, amused and if I'm honest, a little turned on.

"Which one you prefer," he says huskily.

"Hmm." I tap my index finger to my chin pretending to mull over my decision. We both know I want the bad boy. Lucas is sexy as hell with all his bulging muscles and tattoos. We both know it. "Gonna have to pass on that one."

He places his hand over his heart. "You wound me, Addy." He grins a boyish grin that he pulls off flawlessly.

"Wow, moving onto nicknames now, are we?"

He shrugs, nodding to our friends. "Looks like it."

The line moves, and it's my time to order. "Hey, Justin, you want one?" I point to the teenage boy waiting to take my order.

"Yes." He reaches for his wallet, but I wave him off.

"What about you?" I turn to look at Lucas. His wallet is already out, and he's handing money over for four large lemonades before I can protest. "Here." I try to hand him some money, but he glares at my hand.

His answer is to hand each of us our lemonades. "Now what?" he asks.

"We're starving," Harper blurts, then blushes.

"Lead the way," Justin says as they move on to the next booth with Lucas and I stepping in behind them.

We end up getting walking tacos, finding a nearby picnic table to sit and eat. "Have either of you ever been here?" I ask the guys.

They both nod. "A few times," Justin confesses.

"It's a shame it only happens once a year," Harper speaks up. "Then again, it's probably a good thing. I would want to eat here every day. That's not good for the figure," she says, blushing.

It's an anomaly for me, seeing her like this. Harper is usually the most outspoken of the two of us, and I've seen her blush more today than I have the entire time I've known her. Well, it seems that way at least. We've been thick as thieves since preschool That's how I know she's really into him. I've been there, so I know the rush of finding a guy you click with. However, for me, it always ends in some kind of drama, and I'm exhausted just thinking about it.

"Someone is looking out for us, Harper," I say, laughing.

"Right?" She turns to Justin and Lucas. "You guys plan on sticking around? There's a concert later," she tells them.

"Anyone we know?" Justin asks her.

"It's a cover band. Addy and I saw them a few months ago. They cover pretty much any genre."

"Luke?" Justin asks.

"I'm in."

"Great. How about we walk some of this off?" Harper asks.

"After you." Justin stands from the table and holds his hand out for her.

I do the same gathering our trash. When I turn around, Lucas is standing so close, I bump into him. "What do you say we give them some time?" He motions toward our friends.

"If this is some play to get me alone, you're wasting your time." I say the words, but I must admit, it's a pretty good plan, if that's what this is, for both Justin and Lucas.

"Well, this is a festival of thousands." He grins. "Come on, let's give them some time. They seem to be hitting it off."

"Yeah," I agree. "Harper's really into him."

"That's good to hear. Justin has had a rough time. He needs normal."

"Sounds like my life," I mumble.

"Where to first?" he asks.

I smirk. "You tell me."

A knowing grin crosses his face. "Are you challenging me, Addyson Stafford?"

I shrug. "You think you can hold my interest?"

He leans in close. "You and I both know I can."

Goose bumps break out across my skin. Why does he affect me so much? Why now of all times, when I've declared a break on dating, does he fall into my life? Regardless, I'm sticking to my guns. No dating, nothing serious. This girl needs a break, and so does my heart.

chapter
four

LUCAS

The beautiful Addyson is more affected by me than she lets on. She says she's on a break, but damn if that doesn't make me want to change her mind. It took restraint to not text her this week. I had to keep reminding myself that she says she's not interested and that I was reaching out to her for my boy. Then I saw her today. Her black hair pulled back in a ponytail, exposing her long slender neck. Like now, when I lean in close, I want to trace the column with my tongue, taste her.

"Challenge accepted," I say, tossing my arm casually over her shoulder.

"What did I get myself into?" she asks dramatically, rolling those big brown eyes.

"You, my dear Addy, have just signed on to have the time of your life."

"Wait." She stops walking, which causes me to stop too since I still have my arm over her shoulder. "Should I buy some boots?" She looks up at me.

"Boots? Why would you need boots?"

Her smile is devious. "You know, shit's starting to get deep, and I just had my toes done." Her smile widens to a grin, unable to prevent it even though I know she tried from the twitch of her lips.

"Funny girl." I shake my head.

"I'll be here all night," she quips.

I want to kiss the smile right off her lips, but I'm not about to press my luck. This beauty already has me in the friend zone, no need to make it worse.

"All right, let's see." I look around the festival trying to decide our next move when I see a mechanical bull. "Feeling adventurous?"

"What do you have in mind? I'm not bungee jumping or anything extreme."

"How about a mechanical bull?"

Her eyes light up. "You think you can ride eight seconds?" She lays down the challenge.

"Oh, sweetheart." I smile down at her. Lifting the arm that's not around her shoulders, I flex. "I can ride all night. Question is, can you?" My voice is husky just thinking about her riding me. Her mind must also go straight for the gutter. Her cheeks pink ever so slightly, causing my cock to perk up and take notice. Shifting my feet, I discretely adjust.

"Wouldn't you like to know," she finally fires back.

"We can test that theory. You tell me when you're ready."

"The bull, Lucas." She laughs, sliding out from under my arm and pushing me toward the tent with the mechanical bull.

"Call me whatever you want, Addy, as long as I get to show you."

"Show me up there." She points to the bull.

We get to the tent, and there are two teenagers who are just finishing up. Otherwise, it's just the two of us. "Who's going first?" I ask her.

"You."

I nod and hand the attendant my five dollars. "Hold this." I hand her my phone and wallet, and head toward the gate. Sure, it's unorthodox to give her my wallet, I barely know her, but something in my gut tells me I can trust this girl.

"You ever ride?" the greasy-haired roadie asks me.

"Nope."

"Climb on. You can only hold on with one hand. You stay on for a full eight seconds, you get your money back."

"Easy. It's eight seconds," I boast.

"We'll see about that," Addyson calls out from her spot just outside of the ring.

"Don't distract me, woman," I tease.

She makes a big show of zipping her lips and tossing away the key. Her brown eyes are sparkling with laughter as I climb on and settle myself on the fake bull.

"Wait!" she calls.

The roadie and I both turn to face her. "Should we make a wager?" she asks.

"What do you have in mind?"

"Hmm, you win, drinks are on me the next time we see each other."

"And if you win?" I ask her. I want to tell her I'll make her scream my name all night long no matter which one of us wins, but I bite my tongue. "Drinks are on me."

"Deal." I nod my okay for the roadie. He steps up, making sure my feet are secure. Once satisfied, he takes his place at the controls, and slowly the bull begins to move. It's slow and easy, and I know I've got this in the bag. That is until he picks up the speed. My body is jostled this way and that and I'm struggling to hang on. When the bull spins, I know it's the end for me. I feel myself slipping as I fall into the inflated pillows below. I lie here on the inflatable mat trying to catch my breath. I'm not sure if it's the fall or the laughter, but regardless, I'm winded.

"Five seconds," the roadie boasts.

"That. Was. Awesome," Addyson cheers through her laughter. "I-I recorded it." She bites down on her lip to hide her amusement and all I can think about is my teeth replacing hers.

"Let's see what you've got," I say, handing the attendant five dollars for her ride.

She hands me my phone and wallet, then hands me her purse. "It's go time." She bounces into the ring as if she's done this a thousand times.

I watch as the roadie's gaze roams her, his creepy eyes eating her up. "Hey," I call out and they both turn. "She's mine," I tell him, giving him a look that lets him know I was watching and will continue to do so. Addyson looks confused, but the look quickly disappears as the roadie faces her and gets straight to business. I hear him ask her if she needs help climbing on, and I'm ready to jump this wall to help her, but she waves him off. She grabs the horn of the saddle and swings her legs over like a pro.

The bull starts to move, her hand goes in the air, and she's smiling. When the bull pitches to the side, and she goes flying off, I jump over the wall, her purse in hand and rush to her.

"Hey, you can't do that," the roadie scolds me.

I give him a look that dares him to stop me. "Addy," I say, rubbing her back. She's lying on her belly on the inflatable mat shaking. "Addy, hey, tell me what's wrong?" I ask, starting to freak the hell out. "Addyson," I say. This time she must hear something in my voice. She rolls over, and what I thought were tears causing her to sob is laughter.

"I have to do that again." She grins up at me.

Standing, I offer her my hand and help her from the mat. "You scared the hell out of me," I tell her. "Took five years off my life."

"It's like a big pillow." She laughs.

Snaking my arm around her waist, I pull her into me. "Yeah, but when I saw you flying through the air, my instinct was to protect you," I confess.

She looks up at me under those long eyelashes. "You trying to sweet talk me, Luke?"

"Nicknames, huh?" I tease her like she did me earlier.

"That's what friends do." She shrugs.

Right. Friend-zoned. Pulling my wallet out of my back pocket, I hand the attendant a five-dollar bill. "You heard the lady," I tell him. "She wants to go again." Bending down, I whisper in her ear, "Try not to give me a heart attack this time, will ya?"

"I'll see what I can do." She winks and mounts the bull like a pro for the second time.

This time when the roadie makes his way to the controls, I hold my breath. I count the seconds in my head. One one thousand. Two one thousand. Three one thousand. Four one thousand. Five… she slides off the side and lands on the air mat. She's face up and her smile is blinding. I exhale when I see that she's okay and watch as she bounces to her feet.

"You want to go again?" she asks.

"Yeah." I hand over my five dollars when an idea hits me. "We allowed to go at the same time?" I ask the attendant.

He shrugs. "Sure, she's a tiny thing," he says, looking at her.

I hand him another five and pass through the gate. "How do you feel about mixing things up?" I ask her.

"What ya got in mind?"

I bend, placing my lips next to her ear, partly because I love the way she smells. The lavender scent assaults my senses. The other part is I just like being that close to her, and the way she can't hide her reaction to me. "We ride together."

"Is that safe?" she asks, and I can tell by the sparkle in her eye, I've sparked her interest.

"Completely. Give me a second." I walk to the roadie and hand him a twenty. "Take it easy, yeah?" I ask him. He nods, his dirty hands grabbing the twenty and shoving it in his pocket. Walking back to the bull, I climb up just as Chase Rice's "Ride" blares through the speakers. Funny, I didn't even notice there was music until that song started to play. It's sort of fitting considering. Offering my hand to Addyson, she waves me off. I move back, giving her room. Just like the pro she apparently is, she mounts with no problems.

I don't waste any time, sliding up close to her, wrapping one arm around her waist and the other on the horn of the saddle.

"What do I hold onto?" she breathes.

"Place your hand on mine," I whisper. I wait until she does. Then I reach out for her other hand and place it on my thigh. "Hold on tight, Addy." She nods. I pull her back against me, feeling her tight little ass nestled against my cock. I give the roadie a nod, and the bull starts slow and easy as Chase croons through the speakers. She bounces when the bull jerks and I'm hard as steel. What once was a good idea might be an embarrassment when I climb off this bull.

Round and round we turn. And I'm content to have her bouncing on my cock, even through our clothes.

She calls out, "Are you taking it easy on us?"

The roadie nods.

"Don't," she calls out in laughter.

He shrugs, ignoring the fact that I just slipped him a twenty to do just that and turns the knob. We twist faster, front to back, side to side. With each movement, we seem to be moving faster. Addyson's grip on my thigh is tight, but her laughter is anything but. Knowing that we've been on here more than eight seconds due to our slow start, I eye the roadie as he smirks and turns the knob again. We're starting to slip. I release my hold on the saddle and wrap her tightly in my arms, just as we slide off and fall to the inflatable mats. I break her fall, which was my intention, but the breath whooshes out of me as we land.

Her sweet laughter greets me. She rolls over on top of me and smiles. Placing her hands on my chest, she pushes herself up, and now she's straddling me. If she didn't feel how that ride affected me before, she sure as hell does now. Her eyes widen, and the vixen rolls her hips.

"Addyson," I warn her.

"Luke." She grins. "Looks like we both got our eight-second ride." She jumps to her feet. Standing over me, she offers me a hand. I let her pull me up, and when my feet are steady, I pull her into me.

"You need to stay close, but don't touch me," I say just for her. My voice is gruff.

"Everything okay?" she asks sweetly.

I pull her even closer, letting her tight little body align with mine. "I'm pretty sure you already know the answer to that question."

She sucks in a breath. "Yeah," she breathes.

"Time's up," the roadie calls out.

Looking over my shoulder, I glare at him, but it doesn't seem to bother him in the slightest. Turning Addyson around, I keep her close as we exit the ring. "Now where?"

She looks over her shoulder and up at me. "You need a minute?"

"That would be nice."

"Over there." She points to the side of the building. Walking with her tucked in close in front of me, we make our way to the side of the building.

As soon as we're out of sight, I release her and lean back against the wall. My eyes close just as her cell rings. I listen as she talks to I assume Harper, telling her we'll meet them somewhere.

"That was Harper," she tells me when she hangs up. "I guess there's a show before the show. They're saving us seats."

"Seats?"

She laughs. "Translation is they bought a blanket and are offering to share their real estate." Her eyes drop to my dick. "After that." She nods, cheeks blushing.

"Now she blushes," I mumble. I don't bother to hide it when I grip my dick and adjust so I'm more comfortable. "Ready?" I ask, pulling myself from the side of the building.

"You good?"

"I will be."

"You sure?" She eyes my dick again. Her tongue swipes over her lips, and I have to bite back my groan.

"Not if your sexy ass keeps looking at me like that."

"Y-you think my ass is sexy?" Her question isn't coy or her begging for compliments. It's as if she doesn't understand how incredibly gorgeous she is.

I nod. "As fuck," I admit. No shame. Her cheeks are now a nice rose color.

"We better go," she says, turning on her heel and walking away.

In a couple of long strides, I catch up with her, once again throwing my arm over her shoulder. I must admit this is a first for me, being friend-zoned. I'm not really feeling it. I wish I could punch all those other assholes who'd met her before me. They've fucked me over with this one.

chapter
five

Addyson

I need a minute, one I don't get because Lucas and his long-ass legs catch up with me in no time. Now his arm is slung over my shoulders as we walk toward the hill where Harper and Justin are waiting for us. Who would have thought that riding a mechanical bull would turn into... that? I can honestly say I've never been more turned on in my life.

Lucas Prescott is lethal.

"Over there." Lucas points with the hand that's not wrapped around my shoulders. He guides us effortlessly through the crowd. When we reach the blanket, Harper's eyes widen seeing his arm around me. I give a subtle shake of my head telling her not to bring it up. Lucas releases me, and motions for me to sit first. I take the spot next to Harper, who also just happens to be sitting really close to Justin. Lucas settles next to me. His arm holds him up, braced behind me on the blanket.

"What did y'all get into?" Justin asks.

"We rode a bull," Lucas boasts.

"No shit?" Justin asks, surprised.

"It was a mechanical bull," I clarify.

Justin and Harper both laugh. "I would have loved to have seen that," Justin says.

"Well, today just so happens to be your lucky day." I pull my phone out of my pocket and show them the video I took of Lucas's first ride.

"Oh, I've got one too." He laughs, pulling out his phone showing my video. I just roll my eyes and laugh with him. If you can't beat them, join them. Isn't that how the saying goes? Besides, it was a good time.

"We should do it," Justin tells Harper.

"Yeah, y'all could ride together," Lucas offers. "We did."

Harper's eyes go wide, and they're full of questions, which thankfully, she keeps to herself for the time being. I know my best friend. There's no way I'm getting out of giving her the details. That would be too easy.

"Eight seconds," I tell them. "If you stay on for eight seconds you get your money back."

"How much is it?" Harper asks.

"Five dollars."

"Is it worth all that?" she asks.

I think about my solo ride, and then the ride we did together. The way his body wrapped around mine, my hand digging into his thigh, and other things. "Mmmhmm," I say, not even realizing it. Harper and Justin crack up laughing. I chance a glance at Lucas, partly to hide my embarrassment from our friends and to gauge his reaction.

"Should I tell him how good it feels to have your ass pressed against my cock?" he whispers. A shiver races through me despite the warm summer temperatures.

Holy hell. Any other time, I'd be shouting a guy down so damn fast for saying such a thing, especially a guy I barely know. But... Lucas. Honest to God, he has me reacting and behaving in ways I never saw coming. "Lucas," I scold lightly, smacking his leg. He throws his head back and laughs.

Luckily, the opening act begins to play, and all conversation is brought to a halt. We listen as they play five songs, straight through. We're all just relaxing, enjoying the show as if we've hung out like this a million times.

At intermission, Lucas stands. "I'm going to grab a drink, want anything?"

"I'll come with you. Harper?" Justin asks.

"Maybe a bottle of water." She reaches for money but he stops her.

"Addy?" Lucas asks.

"I'm good, thanks." With a nod, they walk off into the crowd.

"Addyson, you have about five minutes, because the other five is mine. Start spilling."

"There's nothing to spill." Unless you count the fact that my body is craving his.

"Right, I saw that look on your face."

"Fine," I concede. I give her a quick run-down. "Why now, Harper? Why would I find a guy who makes me feel this way after the second time I've laid eyes on him?"

"That's the way it works. You find what you're looking for when you least expect it."

"No." I shake my head. "I'm on the bench, remember?"

"That's crazy talk. Have you seen him?" she asks.

I give her a look that tells her she damn well knows I've seen and felt him. "My time's up." I look over my shoulder for the guys and don't see them. "What about Justin? The two of you seem to be hitting it off."

"We are. He's such a nice guy," she gushes. "He's interested."

"Uh, yeah." I laugh.

"No, I mean, yes, he is, but it's more than that. He listens. He asks questions about me, about my job. He's interested."

"Lucas assures me he's one of the good ones."

"Funny, Justin told me the same about Lucas."

"I'm sure he is," I say as if it doesn't matter. The truth is it does matter, but I didn't need to hear he's a good guy from Justin through Harper. Lucas is proving that all on his own.

"Here you go." Lucas hands me a bottle of water. "In case you change your mind," he says, taking his seat next to me on the blanket. "I thought we could share." He holds out a large bag of popcorn.

"Can anyone resist popcorn?" I ask, grabbing a handful of the warm, salty, buttery goodness.

"Nope." He winks then grabs a handful for himself.

By the time the main act takes the stage, we've finished off the full bag of popcorn. The crowd roars, and so do Harper and I. When those in front of us climb to their feet, we do too. Justin and Lucas follow us. Song after song, we sing and dance. Harper and I are in our element. We love music, dancing, and concerts. It's all heightened by the two sexy guys who are right there with us never missing a beat. An outsider looking would think we've all been friends for years, not days.

When a slow one comes on, it's completely dark except for the lights from the stage. When Justin pulls Harper into his arms, I smile. She's happy, and he really does seem to be a nice guy.

"Come here," Lucas says, pulling my back to his chest. He wraps his arms around me and slowly, we sway to the beat. This doesn't change anything, but he's hard to say no to. His strong arms wrapped around me feel better than well… anything ever has. As we listen to the band cover "Lost In You" by Three Days Grace, he holds me as if I'm his and he's mine. Too bad my jaded heart knows better.

"My lucky night," he whispers in my ear as another slow song begins to play. This time it's their cover of "Whoever Broke Your Heart" by Murphy Elmore. Lucas surprises me when he begins to sing the words, just for me. His deep voice doesn't miss a note or lyric. That too is surprising. He seems to be a music lover like me. He's been singing every song just as we have all night long. This time though, this time it's more intimate.

The song comes to an end, and Lucas places a kiss on my neck. He loosens his hold on me, but his hands stay on my hips as the band speeds things up. That's how the rest of the night goes. He handles me as if we're together, and even though I know I should protest, I don't. I let him and enjoy every second of it.

"They were good," Justin comments as we fold the blanket and gather our trash.

"Told you," Harper says. "We've seen them a few times. They really can cover everything."

"Do the two of you go to a lot of concerts?" he asks.

"We do. It's kind of our thing." Harper looks over at me, and I nod.

"We're concert junkies. You should see all of our T-shirts." I laugh.

"Favorite genre?" Justin asks, looking at Harper and then me.

"All of it," we say at the same time, causing him to laugh.

"I can see that from the two of you." He takes the now folded blanket from Harper and shoves it under his arm before he slides his hand over hers. "Now where?"

"The bull," Lucas blurts, and Justin grins.

"You riding again?" Harper asks me.

"I think I'll sit this one out, but you should do it. It's a good time."

"We better hurry. This place closes down in an hour."

I want to tell them an hour is plenty of time to take an erotic bull ride, but I keep that little tidbit to myself. They're going to find out soon enough. Lucas guides me through the crowd with his hand on the small of my back. He's affectionate, and normally that would be something I love, but it's making it hard for me to remember that I need a break from dating. Hell, who am I kidding? Looking at the man makes it hard to remember, and when he touches me, my mind goes blank.

The bull tent is empty when we get there. I take the blanket from Justin and pull out my cell phone. Harper goes first on a solo ride, and she only makes it three seconds before she's bucked off. She was laughing hysterically before the bull even started to move so I'm surprised she lasted that long. Justin goes next. He manages a five-second ride before he falls to the ground.

"It's even harder when you ride together," I call out to them.

"That's an understatement," Lucas mutters beside me.

I ignore him, because what do you say to that? Instead, I hold up my phone and hit Record as they mount the bull. I have to bite my lip to keep from laughing when I see Harper's face when Justin pulls her back to his chest.

"We got shafted," Lucas says beside me.

Keeping the camera rolling, I look over. "How so?" I whisper, knowing the camera is picking up our conversation. I'll just have to mute my phone or edit it before I send it to Harper.

"They get to relive it." He points to the camera. "All I have is the memory of what it felt like to have you nestled up against my cock."

He's blunt, and I find that I like it. In fact, I love it. There is no bullshit with Lucas, no sugar-coating things. "I would offer to give it another go, but I'm not sure either of us could handle that." I give him the same honesty. He doesn't say anything, so I turn to look at him. He's watching me, his eyes full of... want. It's intoxicating to have his attention on me. Even more so when the need I feel is mirrored back at me.

"You're dangerous," I whisper.

He leans in close. "Do you realize how badly I want to kiss you right now?" His voice is gruff.

"Tell me," I counter, breathless from just the thought of his lips pressed to mine.

Laughter and the sound of our friends hitting the mat pull our attention. I stop recording, shoving my phone into my back pocket.

"I'd trace your lips with my tongue, taking my time tasting you. I'd pull you close, my hands on your ass, lifting you, giving myself better leverage to slip my tongue past your lips. I'd explore your mouth, Addy. I'd make damn sure you tasted me hours later."

Harper and Justin head our way, causing him to stand back to his full height and pull away. I asked him to tell me, but I wasn't expecting… that.

"Ready?" Harper asks.

"Y-yeah," I say, clearing my throat.

"We'll walk you to your cars."

"Addyson drove," Harper tells them.

Justin takes her hand and offers to take the blanket, but I shake my head. I'm holding it to my chest as if it's my lifeline. In a way, it is. Justin and Harper lead the way as Lucas places his hand on the small of my back and guides me to follow them through the thinning crowd.

"So, I'm glad you found us." I hear Harper say.

"Yeah, and now I have your number." Justin chuckles.

"I hope you use it." She smiles up at him.

My girl is smitten, and I couldn't be happier for her.

"Awe, look what we did," Lucas says, pitching his voice.

"Our babies are growing up," I say overly sweet. Harper and

Justin look over at us and the four of us roll with laughter.

"Be safe," Lucas says, his lips next to my ear.

"Always."

"You know, you should probably text me when you get to your place, just so I don't worry."

He's smiling, but something tells me the intense look in his eyes means he's serious. "I'm a big girl, Luke."

"I know that, Addy, but you're also beautiful and going home late at night on your own."

"Harp," I call out, not taking my eyes off his. "You staying at my place tonight?" I ask her.

"You can just crash at mine," she answers.

"Problem solved."

"Addyson." His tone is a warning.

"Sheesh, fine, I'll text you."

"Thank you." He leans in and wraps his arms around me in a hug. "I had a great time." I try to ignore how my body relaxes into his, how his warmth surrounds me. I ignore how comfortable I feel with him already.

"Me too." He opens the door for me, waiting to shut the door until I'm buckled in. Glancing over, I see Justin is crouched down, head through the open window talking to Harper. I turn back to Lucas giving them space. I'm sure she'll tell me all about it. "Thanks for that." I motion my head toward our friends.

"My buddy gets the girl. I got an eight-second ride. Sounds like a fair trade to me," he says, smiling.

"Goodnight, Luke."

"Night, Addy."

chapter
six

LUCAS

It's been two weeks since the festival. Two weeks of thinking about her dark silky hair, those big brown eyes, and the way her body felt pressed up against mine. Two very long weeks. We've texted back and forth a few times, but she's shut down all my advances. I've offered dinner, a movie, a festival a few towns over, even offered to come to her place and make dinner. No to all of it. That's why I'm currently sitting at my desk tamping down my excitement as Justin waits for my answer.

"Well? Are you in or not?"

"I'm in. When and where?"

"Harper agreed, but she said low-key. She doesn't want the attention."

"How's that feel?" I ask, laughing. "To find a woman who doesn't want the fanfare that comes with the Atwood name?"

He doesn't hesitate. "Fucking fantastic."

I nod. It's still too soon to tell, but Harper seems genuine. I know he's holding back a little as well, but I can see he's really into her. More than anyone since that bitch Amy. "So, Stagger?" I ask him.

"Yeah, that's what I was thinking. That's where we met them after all. Have you talked to Addyson?"

"A few text messages here and there."

"She playing games?" he asks.

"No. She's jaded. I've been friend-zoned."

"That sucks for you, my man. Maybe move on?"

"Nah, not ready for that."

"She's under your skin."

I nod. "So fucking deep."

"After what, two encounters and a few text messages?"

"Hello pot, meet kettle."

He raises his hands in surrender. "Sorry, you're right. It's just Harper and I have hung out half a dozen times already."

"Well, Harper hasn't had the issues that Addy has." I defend her as if she were mine to defend. She's not. Not yet anyway.

"So, what's your plan?" he asks, smirking. He's amused with my quick defense. I can't deny it's out of character for me.

"Plan?"

"Yeah, you going to try and win her over?"

I run my hands over my face. "I don't know, man. I'm not sure any amount of effort is going to get her to change her mind. I've been shot down every time I've attempted. It's been a lot," I tell him.

"I thought you said a few text messages?"

"Well, a few each day," I confess, making him throw his head back in laughter.

"She's making you work for it."

"Fuck, man, I wish that were the case. She's not playing hard to get. If so, I could work with that. She's locked up like a damn vault. At least, she is over the phone. Getting time with her, that's what I need."

"Good. Friday night, Stagger, seven o'clock." He stands to leave. "Harper said she's never had a good relationship. Every guy she's ever been with has shit on her one way or the other. I know that's not you, but those scars, they run deep, Luke."

"I know."

"All right, man, get your lazy ass back to work." He waves and walks out of my office.

I hesitate for maybe thirty seconds before grabbing my phone and texting her.

> **Me:**   How's your day?

To my surprise, she replies immediately.

> **Addyson:** Going good. Yours?

Small talk. I need to get us past this. I need her to get to know me. I've never felt the attraction that I feel with her. We owe it to ourselves to explore it.

> **Me:**   Just missing you.
>
> **Addyson:** Laying it on thick there, Prescott.
>
> **Me:**   What you see is what you get, sweetheart.
>
> **Addyson:** If I had a dollar for every time a guy has told me that.
>
> **Me:**   I guess I just have to show you.
>
> **Addyson:** You think you can?
>
> **Me:**   Yes.

No point in beating around the bush. I really think I can show her. It's going to take some time, but I have a feeling, one deep in my gut, she's worth it. I've always followed my gut instinct and I'm not going to stop now.

> **Addyson:** Enjoy the rest of your day, Luke.

Me: You too, Addy.

I toss my phone back on my desk and make myself focus on the designs in front of me. Two more days, I remind myself. Two more days until I see her in the flesh. I hope she's ready.

***

Two days later, I'm walking into Sagger fifteen minutes early. I spot Justin at a booth in the back, the same booth the girls were sitting at the night we met them.

"Hey, man," he says as I slide into the booth across from him.

"They on their way?"

"Yeah, Harper was stopping to pick Addyson up."

"Did you get the final plans for the Covington project?" I ask him. I was in meetings all day and didn't hear if they finalized the most recent set of plans.

"Yeah, right as I was leaving the office. I figure I'll take a look at it at some point this weekend."

"Took them long enough," I say. We've been working on this project for over a year. It's a custom home, and Mrs. Covington keeps changing her mind.

"Let's hope it's finished, so we can send it to the builder and be done with it."

"Right? Now I know why Robert told them our build teams were booked solid. He wasn't kidding."

"Look at you boy scouts," Addyson's voice greets me. I look over at her. "If you're trying to score brownie points, it's working," she teases, sliding into the booth next to me.

"Hey, Harper," I greet her friend who waves then gives all her attention to Justin. I turn to look at Addyson. Her dark hair hangs loosely over her shoulders, the silky strands begging for me to bury my hands in it. "How was your day, dear?" I ask her.

"Long," she sighs. "I have a little girl I've been working with for months, and just as she shows progress, something happens at home to set her back. I had to talk to CPS today. They have to get her out of there."

"Sounds tough."

"Yeah. I love my job. Speech therapy was something I had to do as a kid, and my therapist was the best. That's what led me to follow in her footsteps. For the most part, it's straightforward, but there are those kids who you see starting to come out of their shell, and then bam, they clam right up again. That's the bad part of the job."

"Sounds like you could use a drink."

"Definitely. Harp, I'll go. What do you want?"

"Surprise me," Harper tells her.

"You guys need anything?"

"I'll come with you." I go to follow her out of the booth, but she puts her hands up stopping me.

"I can manage, Prescott. Tell me what you want." I love this feisty side of her.

"Two bottles of bud," Justin answers for me.

Asshole.

"I'll be back." She smiles and saunters off to the bar. Every motherfucker in here watches her.

"You're about to break a molar," Justin jokes.

I ignore him and keep my eyes locked on her. It's not until a soft hand covers mine that I turn away. "Hey." Harper smiles. "She's a big girl. She can handle herself."

"She shouldn't have to," I grit out.

"That may be, but she always has. Addyson has had the worst luck with men. We laugh about it, but it's changed her. The harder you shove, the harder she does."

"Trust me, I know," I grumble.

"Here you go," Addyson says a few minutes later. She sets four bottles of beer on the table and takes her seat next to me.

"Straight outta the bottle, huh?" I ask her.

"Is there any other way?"

"Depends, are you asking the current me or the broke college student me?"

"I'm certain our answers are going to be the same. College was stale beer from a keg and cheap wine."

"Not much of a wine drinker, at least not back then," I confess.

"Do you have a choice in college?" She chuckles. "I mean, cheap wine and cheap beer are what it's all about, right?"

"Among other things."

"Right, I'm sure you were one of those looking for a new hookup every night."

"Not every night. I wasn't an angel, but I can guarantee you I know where my dick has been."

She looks over the table at Justin. "You'll give me the dirt, right?" She bats those long eyelashes at him.

"No dirt." Justin shrugs. "He was a nose to the grindstone kinda guy. Didn't party too hard, and he was... selective." He turns to look at Harper. "We both were. Are," he adds as an afterthought.

"So, Harper." I raise my beer to her. "Congrats on the new job."

"Thank you." Her smile is wide.

Justin lifts his beer with one hand and places the other around her shoulders. Instead of congratulating her where we can hear, he leans down and whispers something just for her. Her smile remains, but her blush tells me more than I need to know.

"Oh, Addy, I forgot to tell you, guess who's coming to town?" Harper asks excitedly.

"Santa Clause?" Addy smirks.

"Ha ha, smartass. No, Dan + Shay. I tried to get us tickets, but they're already sold out."

"What? Already? That's crazy."

I look over at Justin, and he gives me a subtle nod. He's definitely thinking what I'm thinking.

"Big Dan + Shay fan?" he asks Harper.

"We both are," she tells him. This time it's Justin's eyes finding mine, and I'm the one giving him a subtle nod.

Justin has connections, like tickets-to-a-sold-out-concert connections. With a phone call, he can make it happen, and I know without a doubt he's going to.

A couple of hours later, after the girls have tossed back more drinks than I can count, we're sliding out of the booth to head home. I stopped at two beers hours ago. I noticed Justin did the same, the ladies however indulged themselves. "How are you getting home?" I ask Addyson.

"Harp drove." She looks up at me. Her eyes are glassy, and she is, without a doubt, in no shape to drive.

"I'm taking them home," Justin says. "I'll bring Harper back in the morning to get her car."

"Does that mean you're staying?" Harper asks him, wrapping her arms around his waist.

"Yeah, I can't leave you alone like this."

"Hel-lo." Addyson waves her hand in the air. "I'll be there." She points to her chest.

"How about I take you home?" I offer. I'll take any chance I can to be alone with her, even if she's passed-out cold. In fact, that idea sounds more and more appealing. I can memorize her features. I don't know when I'll see her again, and that bothers me. It's a new development, but it's only Addyson. No one before her has ever brought these kinds of feelings out of me.

She taps her index finger to her chin and wobbles on her feet. Reaching out, I settle my hands on her hips to steady her. "No f-funny business, mister sexy and I know it."

I don't even try to hold in my laughter.

"It's not funny," she scolds. "You're just like that song." She turns to her best friend. "Harp, who sings that song? That sexy and I know it song, that's Lucas." She leans in and rests her head against my chest.

Harper is pretty much in the same position. "Laugh my fucking ass off." Harper giggles.

"LMFAO," Justin translates for her.

"Yeah." Addyson points toward them, but her face is still buried in my chest. "This guy." She lays her palms flat against my chest. "He's sexy and he knows it."

I bite down on my lip, holding back my laughter. "Let's get you home, funny girl," I tell her.

"I'll get her home," I assure Justin.

"Thanks, man." With extreme patience, we manage to help the girls stagger out of Stagger, the name suddenly fitting the establishment perfectly.

I help her into my truck and her eyes immediately close as she rests her head against the seat. I take a minute to study her. She looks like an angel with her porcelain skin and all that sexy-as-fuck hair of hers. Carefully, I close the door, closing her inside.

She's still sleeping peacefully when I pull up to her condo. Reaching for her purse, I dig around until I find her keys. Throwing her purse over my shoulder, I exit the truck, and carefully open her door. Making quick work of unlatching her seat belt, I lift her into my arms.

"Smell good," she mumbles.

"You think so?" I ask her, amused.

"Mmm," is her reply.

I'm not sure how I do it, but I manage to get the door unlocked and both of us inside her condo without dropping her. Kicking the door shut, I drop her keys on the floor and use my elbow to flip the light switch. I take in my surroundings — living room, kitchen, small dining area, and a dark hallway. I head in that direction, stopping to look in the first room, which appears to be a bathroom. The next door on the opposite side of the hall is a bedroom, but it's sparse. I keep walking to the door at the end of the hall. When I push open the door, I know immediately it's her room. Her lavender scent engulfs me.

Making my way to the bed with nothing but the glow of the moonlight to guide me, I step cautiously. When my knees hit the bed, I carefully lay her on the soft mattress. Reaching over to the nightstand, I turn on the lamp, which casts a soft, warm glow in the room.

Her eyes flutter open, and she stares up at me. "Luke?"

"You're home," I tell her. "Let's get these shoes off you." Stepping to the end of the bed, I work on unstrapping one sandal, then the other from her feet. She wiggles her teal-painted toes once I'm done.

"Harper?" she asks.

"Justin's with her."

"He's nice."

"Yeah," I agree. He is my best friend after all. Leaving her on the bed, I make my way back to the kitchen for a bottle of water and some headache medicine. She's going to need it. I find the medicine in the second cabinet I try, and as I suspected, her fridge is stocked with bottles of water.

"Addyson," I say, sitting on the edge of the bed. "Can you wake up for me? I need you to take these."

"Just say no to drugs, Luke," she slurs. She's going for scolding me, but she fails miserably.

"Just say no. Got it. Can you sit up for me?" I stand and help lift her off the bed.

"Oh," she moans. "That's —" she swallows hard, and I know what's next.

With quick reflexes, I scoop her up in my arms and rush to

the en-suite bathroom. She's barely on her feet before she's dropping to her knees and losing the contents of her stomach. I scramble to hold back her hair, while gently caressing her back.

"Ugh," she groans, resting her head on the edge of the toilet.

"You good now?" I ask her.

"You should go. This isn't sexy."

"You're sexy." She is. Even in this moment, I've never seen anyone more beautiful than her.

"I'm done," she says, attempting to stand.

I release her silky strands, stand, and lift her into my arms. "I've got you."

"You're taking care of me?" she questions.

"Looks like it."

"Thank you."

I set her back on the bed, and she falls back against the pillows. "I'm going to go grab a trash can." I don't even know if she hears me. Her eyes are closed and her breathing is deep and even. Grabbing the trash can from the bathroom, I place it next to the bed. "Addyson, I need you to take these for me." Sliding my arm under her, I lift her up. Her eyes pop open.

"Sleepy."

"I know, beautiful, but you need to take these. You'll thank me in the morning. I promise." She nods, which is more of letting her head fall forward. When she lifts it back up, her mouth is open like a baby bird. I toss the pills into her mouth and hold the open bottle of water to her lips. I slowly pour some into her mouth, and she swallows. "One more drink. The more water we get in you, the better." She opens again, and I pour more water into her mouth. This time once she swallows, she falls back against the bed and groans. Placing the lid back on the bottle, I set it on the nightstand.

"You need anything?" I ask, pushing the hair out of her eyes.

"The room is spinning," she says, rolling over to her belly.

"It'll stop. Just breathe through it." Gently, I run my fingers up and down her back. Several minutes pass, and from her silence, I'm assuming she's asleep. I debate on what I should do. I hate leaving her here like this all alone. What if something happens? Eyeing the chair in the corner of the room, I decide to stay for a couple of hours just to make sure she's going to be okay. Making my way back out to the living room, I pick up the keys that I dropped, setting them on the small table just inside the door. I lock the door, kick off my shoes, turn off the lights, and head back to her room.

chapter
seven

Addyson

There's a jackhammer in my head. That's the only logical excuse for the way my head is throbbing. Slowly, I peel open one eye at a time, testing my vision. I blink a few times until the room comes into focus. My mouth tastes like I ate a dead animal, and I'm dry as if I'd been sucking on cotton. "Why did I drink so much?" I whine, rolling over on my side. I see a bottle of water and I reach for it, twisting off the cap and lifting my head only high enough off the pillow to drink greedily.

"You might want to slow down," a deep voice warns, causing me to scream and drop the bottle of water. Thankfully, it was almost empty.

"What are you doing here?" I ask as my heart leaps in my chest. Why is he in my room?

He sits up from the chair in the corner and stretches his arms over his head. "I brought you home. You were pretty messed up. I was just going to stay a couple of hours and make sure you were okay. I fell asleep." He shrugs.

"Thank you." Slowly I sit up in bed. "Harper?" I ask him. I can only imagine what I look like. I might not be interested in dating anyone, but when there's a man, a sexy man like Lucas Prescott in your room the morning after you pass out drunk, a girl frets over her appearance.

"Justin took care of her."

"I hope I wasn't awful," I say, hiding my face behind my hands. He chuckles. "How bad?" I ask, dropping my hands.

"Not too bad. You got sick, which is why I stayed to make sure you were okay."

"I never drink like that. One time in college and I swore I'd never do it again."

"You were celebrating."

"Yeah." I smile, thinking about my best friend and her promotion. She's busted her ass to get where she is.

I watch as he stands and stretches again. His T-shirt rises, and I can clearly see his toned abs. "Addyson," he says sternly. My eyes pop up to his. "You can't look at me like that," he growls.

"Like what?" Yeah, I'm playing the denial card.

"Like you want me. I'm a man, and you're sitting there all sexy from sleep. I only have so much restraint."

I open my mouth to speak, but my words seem to be lodged in my throat. "I—"

"Get moving. I'm going to borrow some toothpaste. Then I'm taking you to breakfast."

"Lucas, no, you've already done too much," I protest. It's weak at best. The more time I spend with him, the more I want to be around him. Slowly, I can feel my resolve start to crumble.

"Fine, you can take me to breakfast." He grins as he heads toward the bathroom.

"There are extra toothbrushes under the sink," I call out. I always get them when I go to the dentist, and I have one of those fancy electric ones. Harper has used my stash more times than I can count.

"Thanks, now get moving," he calls out through the bathroom door.

"You're in my bathroom."

"I'll be done in a minute," he calls back.

Climbing out of bed, I gather some clothes and wait for him to come out of the bathroom. "All yours," he says a few minutes later when he steps out.

Twenty minutes later, we're climbing into his truck and headed toward the local diner. "Sorry about last night. I promise that's not me."

He glances over at me before turning his eyes back on the road. "No need. We've all been there."

"Regardless, you didn't have to take care of me. And… sleep in the chair in my room."

"It was nothing."

"No, it was something. Thank you." He could have gotten in bed with me, taken advantage of me, but he didn't. He could have left me there on my own, but he cared enough to make sure I was okay. A little piece of my hardened heart thaws at that realization.

He nods as he pulls his truck in front of the diner and kills the engine. "Nothing like greasy food for a hangover."

"Ummm… I'm thinking pancakes." I grin.

"The lady wants pancakes, pancakes she shall have." He opens his door and climbs out of the truck. I do the same, meeting him on the sidewalk. He places his hand on the small of my back, like he's done every time I've been with him. His touch is warm, and to my surprise, not unwelcome. Guiding us to the door, he reaches in front of me and opens it, ushering me inside.

"So, tell me more about your job," he asks, relaxing back into the booth. We both just ordered a huge stack of pancakes with a side of bacon.

"I love it. I was in speech therapy as a kid, and my therapist, Miss Susie, she was amazing. She made an embarrassing, difficult situation fun. I want to be that for someone."

"Do you still talk to her?"

"I do actually. In high school, we had to do this project on where you see yourself in five years. Then you had to find someone in that field and shadow them for a day. I reached out to Susie, and that day I spent with her sealed my fate."

"Full circle." He smiles.

"What about you? Did you always want to be an architect?"

He nods. "Yeah, well, I loved to draw and knew I wanted to work with my hands. My grandfather was a carpenter, and I spent a lot of time with him growing up. I was good at math, so I loaded up on algebra, trigonometry, and calculus. My teacher, Mr. Harris, suggested I consider college and focus on architecture, I promised him I'd check it out." He laughs. "My parents were thrilled, and Mom got to work finding schools nearby, and the next week, we went on a visit. I loved the campus was close to home, and the rest is history. Well, unless you want to talk about the SAT and Act testing or there's the GRE and GMAT testing and of course there's my design portfolio."

"Full circle." I beam at him. "Sounds like at a young age you had it all together. How long have you known Justin?"

"I guess you could say that," he says, taking a drink. "We met my freshman year of college. He was in the same program, and we hit it off. He graduated a year before me and helped me get a spot as an intern at his firm, well, our firm." He takes another drink of his orange juice. "You and Harper are tight," he comments.

"Yeah. Pre-school." I can't hide my grin. "We were both terrified and got seated next to each other. We had to turn to our neighbor and introduce ourselves. We've been close ever since."

"Here you go." Our waitress sets two huge plates of pancakes and bacon in front of us. "I'll be right back with some refills," she says, then scurries off.

"I'm never going to be able to eat all of this," I say, looking at the huge stack in front of me.

"Eat what you want. I'll take care of the rest."

"You can't be serious." I look wide-eyed at the amount of food.

He grins. "I'm a growing boy." He pats his flat stomach.

He must work out because those abs I saw earlier, those don't appear from eating big plates of pancakes every day. "How often do you work out?" I blurt.

He shrugs. "Every day." He takes a big bite of his breakfast.

I almost tell him that it shows. I almost tell him that his hard work is paying off. Instead, I shove my mouth full of pancakes and keep my thoughts to myself.

Breakfast is great. We talk about our jobs, college, our families… the conversation never seemed to fizzle out. It's why I'm sitting here in his truck, waiting to go inside my condo, but I can't seem to make myself open the door.

"What are you getting into tonight?" he asks.

"Nothing much. I have some laundry and patient charting to catch up on."

"Why don't you let me take you out to dinner?"

"Luke, you just fed me breakfast." I offered him money, but he wasn't having it.

"Yeah, and I'd like to feed you dinner too."

"Thank you for breakfast and for taking care of my drunk ass last night, but I'm going to have to pass." Reaching for the handle, I open the door and climb out. "I'll see you around, Lucas Prescott." He's too charming and sweet, and easy on the eyes. I can feel myself slipping, wanting to spend more time with him. I can't let myself fall again. Not yet. I need this break. At least that's what I keep telling myself.

"You can plan on it, Addyson Stafford." His voice is husky. Promising.

I feel his eyes on me all the way to my condo, and it sparks a fire inside of me. I almost turn around and tell him I changed my mind about dinner. Almost. Instead, I keep my head held high. My resolve sets and I disappear behind the door. Once inside, I peer through the blinds and watch him drive away. After dropping my purse on the table, I lie down on the couch, closing my eyes. Everything about Lucas screams "date me." I wish I'd met him sooner. I wish I'd met him before my heart was mangled into such a web of lies and pain, before I was broken. My phone rings, pulling me out of my thoughts.

"Hey," I greet Harper.

"How are you feeling?" She sounds as if she's whispering. My guess is that she has a killer headache. She always does after drinking too much.

"Good, how about you?"

"Headache from hell," she says, confirming my suspicion.

"Justin got you home okay?"

"Yeah," she sighs happily. "He stayed. How about you? That's why I'm calling. Justin said Lucas took you home."

"He did. He stayed," I confess. "It's not what you think." I rush to tell her. "He slept in the chair in my room. I guess I was throwing up and he was worried about me. Said he was going to stay a little longer to make sure I was all right and ended up falling asleep in the chair."

"Is he still there?"

"No. We uh… went to breakfast and he just dropped me off."

"Addyson Grace, are you forgetting to tell me something?"

"Nope. That's it. Breakfast. He asked me to dinner, but I said no."

"What?" she screeches, then groans from her headache. "Why would you say no?" she asks, back to her whispering.

"Because," is my reply. It's a shitty one, but I can't seem to put into words that I like Lucas. I can't admit it aloud. I need this break, this time for me. I need to regroup. You can only knock a girl down so much before she has a hard time getting back up. Looking back, all the guys I've dated have been charming and easy on the eyes, just like Lucas. There is nothing different, and I need different.

"Addyson, you can't let the fear of the unknown hold you back."

"That's just it," I confess. "He's sexy and charming and so were they. Lucas is a great guy. In fact, if I had met him sooner, maybe things would have been different."

"They still can be."

"Possibly, but I need to do me for a while. Blake...." I trail off, knowing I don't need to explain what he did to me. He was good to me, doting in fact. I thought for sure my bad luck had been broken. Then we ran into his wife. I've never been more humiliated. Obviously, my judgment is not the best when it comes to men. So, no matter how good of a guy I think he is, there is always that chance he's just putting on a show like the rest of them.

"Take some time. I get it. Promise me you won't stay closed off forever."

"One day," I tell her, unable to make any promises. I refuse to lie to my best friend. We talk for a few more minutes, until Justin gets back to her place with lunch. They're spending the day together. Although I feel a pang of jealousy, I'm so incredibly happy for them. One day I hope to find that. Find trust again and open my heart to love.

One day.

chapter
eight

LUCAS

It's Monday morning and I'm at the office early. Over an hour earlier than usual. Other than Saturday morning with Addyson and my trip to the gym both days, I stayed around my house all weekend. Not that there is anything wrong with that. In fact, I love my house. I've lived there for about three months now. I designed it and had one of the crews build it. It's my dream house. My mom tried to convince me to wait until I find my future bride, as she called it, to build. I considered it, but I was tired of wasting money on my condo rental. I was ready for my own place, and I refused to stop life while I waited for the woman of my dreams to walk into my life.

Little did I know I would soon meet the one and only Addyson Stafford. I can't help but wonder if she would like my house. Maybe one day I'll find out. My mom would love her.

"What are you doing here so early?" Justin asks from the doorway of my office, pulling me out of my thoughts.

"Just getting a jump start on the week." It's not a lie. I just leave out that I sat around all weekend thinking about Addyson and how I can convince her to give me a shot. Pathetic I know, which is why I'm keeping that sliver of information to myself.

He gives me a look that tells me he's not buying what I'm selling. "So, I heard back from Tabitha," he says, stepping inside my office and taking a seat across from me.

"And?"

He grins. "Four tickets, backstage passes, meet and greet."

"Yeah? The girls are going to be stoked." I pull out my wallet. "How much?" I don't care what it costs. She wants to go, and I want to be the one to get her there.

He waves me off. "They were free."

"Come on, man, I'll pay for me and Addyson." No way am I letting him foot the bill for this.

"I'm telling you they were free. It's amazing what money and a prestigious last name will get you. Some people bust their ass and scrimp and save to afford to go to a concert. I make a phone call, and we're hooked up like celebrities for free." He shakes his head in disgust. Justin doesn't like to use his family's money to get a leg up. The fact that he reached out for these tickets tells me exactly how much he likes Harper.

"I know you hate using the family name," I comment. Justin works hard and has a trust fund that will make your head spin from counting all the zeros. He hides it well. At least he tries to, that bitch Amy knew what she was doing. He dodged a bullet with that one.

"Yeah, but Harper really wants to go. I can't wait to tell her. We should tell them together." I can already see he has an idea brewing in his head.

He's not going to get an argument from me. "When is the concert?"

"Next month." He rattles off the date. "I guess he added this date so the ticket sale date and the event are close. Hell, he sold out in ten minutes."

Grabbing my phone, I add it to my calendar. "When do you want to tell them?" Please say tonight, I chant in my head.

"I was thinking about having everyone over to my place this weekend, throw some burgers on the grill."

That means I have to wait all week to see her again. It's not tonight, but it's sooner than I would have seen her otherwise, so I'll take it. "I'm in. You tell me when and where."

I know I answered too quickly when he asks, "What's going on with you and Addyson?"

"Nothing. Not for lack of trying. She's been burned so many times, she's closed off." She's so fun to be around though. Our banter excites me, just as much as her smile or the sound of her laugh.

"What? The Lucas Prescott charm isn't working?"

I can't help but laugh. "She likes me. I can see it in her eyes. But she's not budging. I tried to get her to have dinner with me Saturday night, and she said no." I don't tell him that I texted her a few hours after, but she turned me down again. I even offered to bring dinner to her. No luck.

"I can't really say I blame her. Don't you remember her stories that first night? She's had some pretty shitty luck. Not just that, but I'm sure there was more she wasn't telling us. I mean, she was laughing and joking about it, but it's deep, especially if she's closing off like she is."

"Yeah, I have my work cut out for me, that's for sure." The thought of all those guys, using her like that pisses me off. Were they really that blind to what they had right in front of them? How could they have just used her and thrown her away like that?

He studies me. "You're still pursuing her?"

I nod. "Yeah. She's so laidback, and… normal, for lack of a

better word. She's just Addyson. She's not afraid to order what she wants to eat and makes no apologies for eating it. She's got a great personality. She's sexy as hell." I stop, realizing I'm rambling on about her. I could go on and on about how she has me twisted up in knots. She's genuine and beautiful, and hopefully one day she'll be mine.

"You're hooked."

Rubbing my hands over my face, I exhale. "Yeah, looks like it."

"Is it just the chase?"

"No." I shake my head adamantly. "She's unlike anyone I've ever met."

"Going to be an uphill battle, my friend."

"Don't I know it. Hey, you have to help me. If you get any intel from Harper, send it my way."

"Not unless Harper says I can tell you."

"What? Where's your loyalty?" I razz him. Not that I blame him. Sure, he's my best friend, but I know him well enough to know he's in this for the long haul with Harper. While I'm his best friend, she's his future, his heart. You stay loyal to that.

He shrugs, holding up his little finger. "She's got me, man. It's fucking terrifying with my past experiences, but Harper..." He smiles. "She's worth the risk, you know?"

Yeah, I know. "So you setting this little shindig up with your girl?"

"Yeah, I'll text her now. It's getting *your* girl to agree to tag along that we have to worry about."

My girl. If only I could be so lucky. "Why don't you text Addyson first?" Surely, it will be hard for her to say no to Justin.

He ponders the idea. "That could work. I could tell her I want to get to know Harper's best friend a little better, which is true. I'll just leave out the fact that you're going to be there."

KAYLEE RYAN | 69

I hate that I agree with him. Not that Addyson is avoiding me. But knowing I'm going to be there might sway her decision to pass on the invitation. I just don't know at this point.

"Let me know," I say as he stands. I want to tell him to text her now, here in my office, but I hold back. He'll tell me.

"Send me her number," he says before walking out of my office.

Grabbing my phone, I send him a text with her number, then pull up her name and send her a message as well. Can't have her forgetting about me.

Me: Have a great day, Addy.

Addyson: Thanks. You too, Luke.

I decide to press my luck a little.

Me: Dinner this week?

Addyson: I have a crazy week.

Me: This weekend?

Addyson: Probably not the best idea.

Me: I'll change your mind.

Addyson: You think so?

Me: I know so.

Addyson: You're relentless.

Me: What can I say? I know what I want.

Addyson: I take it you're talking about me?

Me: Yes.

Nothing like laying it all out on the line. I'm not going to hide because she's not ready. I just need to prove to her that when she's ready, I'll be here. I meant what I told Justin. I've never met anyone like her.

She doesn't reply, and I'm sure I've stunned her speechless. Good. She needs to know where I stand.

I hope she's ready soon.
I'm pursuing her.
I'll show her I'm the difference.

chapter
nine

Addyson

I was surprised to get a text from Justin earlier this week asking me to his place for a cookout. He claimed he had a surprise for Harper, and that he thought it would be nice if the two of us got to know each other better. I must admit that won him some major brownie points. I get that they're together, but one fact remains, she will *always* be my best friend. So for him to reach out, how could I say no to that?

He assured me it's low-key at his place. He also has a pool, so he told me to bring my suit. I wanted to ask him if Lucas was going to be there, but I held strong. Part of me wants him to be and the other part, the part that finds it increasingly difficult to ignore my attraction to him, that part hopes he's not there. Don't ask me which one is stronger.

After shoving my swimsuit, sunscreen, towel, and cover-up into a bag, I'm ready to go. I text Harper and let her know I'm on my way. Grabbing my purse and keys, I lock up and head out to my car. I punch the address Justin sent me into the GPS on my phone and I'm on my way. It's a beautiful day. The sun is shining and sitting poolside with some burgers and company sounds like the perfect day.

I turn down the radio when my GPS tells me I'm arriving at my destination. A weird habit I've picked up over the years. Turning into the drive, I'm in awe of the two-story home. It's well landscaped and exactly what I would expect for someone like Justin to be living in. He seems as though he has it together. No games. No dishonesty. For my best friend's sake, I hope he's the real deal, just as he seems to be.

Tearing my eyes off the house, I focus on where I'm going. That's when I see it. Lucas's truck is parked in the drive, Harper's car next to it. Nerves take flight, and it's as if there are a million butterflies dancing around in my stomach. I shouldn't be excited to see him. I don't want to be excited to see him. That's the lie I continue to tell myself.

After pulling in behind Harper, I put the car in park and pull the keys from the ignition. I take my time turning off the GPS on my phone and checking my email. I'm stalling, hoping the butterflies calm down before I actually set eyes on him. I take a slow deep breath in and gradually exhale before gathering my bag, and climbing out of the car. Harper told me to come on around back when I arrive, so that's what I do. I follow the manicured sidewalk around the side of the house.

"There she is," Harper calls when she sees me. "I didn't think you'd ever get here."

"Not my fault you're early," I fire back.

"Nope. I woke up here." She grins.

"Hussy," I tease. She gives me a beaming smile. It's been a while since I've seen her so happy.

"Addyson." Lucas stands and reaches for my bag. "Let me take that for you."

"Thanks," I say, handing him my bag.

"What can I get you to drink? Justin pretty much has anything you can think of. I can mix you a drink," he offers.

I raise my hands up. "No, thank you." I laugh. "Besides, I'm driving home."

"I can take you home," he offers, holding up a bottle of water.

"You're more than welcome to stay here, Addyson," Justin offers sweetly.

"Thank you, but water is fine." I watch Lucas as he sets my bag on the table, and plunges his hand into the cooler, pulling out a bottle of water. "Thanks," I say when he hands it to me.

"You have your suit on?" Harper asks.

"No, it's in my bag though."

"I've been waiting for you to get here. We need to catch up." She turns to face Justin. "What are your plans?" she asks him.

"Spending the day with you."

I can visibly see her swooning from this side of the table. Her eyes soften, her shoulders relax, and her smile is bright.

"You," she points to me, "go get changed. We're lounging by the pool and catching up. I haven't seen much of you lately."

"Yes, ma'am." I mock salute her. She's right. We've only talked a few times this week. That's not like us. "Justin, do you mind if I go inside and get changed?"

"I'll show you." Lucas stands and picks up my bag, heading toward the sliding glass door.

"Make yourself at home, Addyson," Justin replies, reaching over and placing his hand on Harper's thigh.

"Addyson," Lucas calls out. He's standing at the door, my bag in his large hands, waiting on me.

I stand from the table and make my way toward him. "I can take that." I reach for my bag.

"You can, but why would you if I'm here?"

His voice is void of any teasing, and his brown eyes are serious. "Because I can take care of myself."

"There's no debate about that. What I'm trying to say and apparently failing to do is that if I'm around, I want to do these things for you."

"Lucas," I start, and he holds up his hand to stop me.

"Let me, Addy. How am I supposed to show you who I really am if you won't let me be me?"

How can I possibly argue with that? More butterflies take flight in my belly. "Thank you," I concede. He wants to show me who he really is, and to my surprise, I can't wait to find out.

He nods. "This way." He pulls open the sliding glass door and motions for me to step inside. I'm immediately assaulted by the cool air of the air conditioning. I startle when Lucas entwines our fingers. I let him guide me through the kitchen and down the hall. "This is his guest quarters. His parents use it when they come to visit. You can leave your stuff in here."

"Wow, this house is great."

"We are architects," he reminds me with a wry grin.

"I know that, but that doesn't mean you can build a home or does it?" I ask him.

He shrugs. "Depends, some of us can draw and design but have no build experience. That's just for the most part. Me, on the other hand, my grandfather was a carpenter, I picked up a few things. That's where my love for building and designing started. It just grew from there."

"Do you have a house like this?" I ask, spinning in circles.

"I have a house that I designed and even did some of the build. The things I had time for. The rest of it I had one of our crews contracted to complete."

"That's amazing. To know you designed every detail, every wall." I trace my hand along the wood trim on the door of the guest quarters.

"You teach people, kids specifically, to talk. That's amazing," he says softly.

"I should probably change."

"Need some help?" he asks, his voice husky.

"N-No, I think I can handle it."

"I'll be in the hall, you know, in case you need help with a zipper or something."

"No zippers."

"Shame." He releases my hand and walks into the hall, softly closing the door behind him.

It's pathetic that all it takes are his brown eyes on me and that deep voice of his to turn me on. It's embarrassing. Tossing my bag on the bed, I dig out my bikini. It's teal, my favorite color. I strip down to nothing, and my body heats thinking about Lucas standing just on the other side of the door. Quickly, I change into my bikini and white cover-up. I collect my towel, sunscreen, my phone, and make sure my sunglasses are still on top of my head, and open the door.

"Jesus," he whispers when he sees me. "Are you trying to torture me, Addy?" He steps toward me. "Tell me, how am I supposed to walk around like this all day?"

I give him a confused look, and he looks down between us. My eyes follow his, and that's when I realize what he's talking about. He's aroused. "For me?" I ask breathlessly. Let me tell you, those swim trunks leave nothing to the imagination.

His arm slides around my waist as he pulls me into him, his erection hitting against my belly. There's nothing but my thin cover-up between us. "You're fucking gorgeous," he whispers, his lips next to my ear.

I shiver from his words and the contact. I take a minute to compose myself before saying, "Does that line usually work for you?"

He sighs heavily. "We better get back out there." He wraps his hand around mine and leads me out of the room.

I know I'm being unfair to him. He's given me no reason to treat him this way. I don't want to, it's just not something I can seem to control. My heart has been battered and bruised. It needs time to heal. However, that's no excuse to be so hard on him. I need to make a conscious effort to not do that. Not to Luke. I follow him, letting him lead me until we reach the sliding glass door. I can see Harper and Justin as they talk, their bodies close. They aren't paying us a bit of attention, but I pull back, making him drop my hand anyway. I can't look at him, so I just reach for the handle, open the door, and step out onto the deck. "Sorry, Justin. I need to steal my bestie for a few hours."

"She's here, that's what matters." He kisses Harper on the temple before backing his chair away from hers, giving her room to stand. She grabs her towel and phone and motions for me to follow her down to the pool.

"What's been going on with you?" Harper asks once we're settled.

We spend the next hour catching up. I tell her about work, and she tells me about her new woes as the manager of the hotel. Justin brought us down two bottles of water with a kiss for Harper without saying a word about twenty minutes ago.

"I say we get in the pool. It's hot as hell out here."

"You don't have to tell me twice."

"Race you," Harper calls, already running toward the water.

"Damn it, Harp." I laugh, chasing after her. I dive in just seconds after her. "You cheated." I pout when we both finally come up for air.

She shrugs unapologetically. "Snooze you lose," she jokes. We swim our way to the edge and rest our arms while kicking our feet. "You've got him chasing his tail," Harper whispers.

"What? Who?" I look over at the guys and find them both watching us.

"Lucas."

"He's a flirt," I tell her. "A gorgeous flirt," I add, laughing.

"That may be, but he's an interested flirt."

If only I could see the future. If I could see that Luke really is one of the good guys. "I told you, I'm on a break. Besides, you and Justin are really hitting it off. When he shits on me, which we both know he will since that's how my story goes, it will make days like this awkward for all of us."

She nods. "I can see that with your experience, but imagine this. What if he turns out to be your prince?"

"I love that you seem to have found yours, but I'll forever be the girl on the bench, watching from the sidelines." My gut twists to think that I'll never find love, never have a family of my own. We can't always get what we wish for.

"You promised," she says sternly.

"Okay, maybe not forever, but Blake wrecked me. He was charming and sweet, and handsome, all the same things that Lucas has. I was with him for months. Months, Harper, and I didn't know he was married. I thought we were building something, and in an instant, it was all torn apart."

"He's a cheating bastard, and you deserve better."

"That's just it. There were no signs, or if there were, I ignored them. Lucas is sexy and smart. He's charming and kind. He's everything I want... or wanted." I quickly correct. "I'm just not sure I have anything in me left to give."

"Give it some more time. You'll get there."

I let her believe that. Me, I'm not so sure. My heart was shattered. While I'm over him, I'm not over the betrayal. Not just his, but all the others as well. I've never had a relationship where I wasn't used or cheated on. A girl can only take so much. Hell, if they dumped me because they were just not feeling it, or fell out of like or love or whatever, I would be able to handle that. Dust myself off and get back on the horse, but this... it's too much. Too painful. I have this constant worry, waiting for the drama to fall into my lap, for the betrayal to be revealed.

Hard pass.

chapter
ten

LUCAS

I've checked more times than I care to admit to make sure I'm not drooling. Lucky for me, Justin is in the same situation with Harper, so he hasn't noticed and therefore isn't giving me shit for it. Not that I'd care at this point. I'm soaking up every second of this time with her. Memorizing the curves of her body in the tiny bikini. I can honestly say it's an image I'll take with me to the grave.

The girls run and jump in the pool. I watch as they swim to the edge, laughing. When they look over and catch me staring, I turn to look at Justin, who averts his gaze toward me.

"Shit." He chuckles. "I can't seem to help it."

"At least she wants you to look."

"Trouble in paradise?" he teases.

I ignore him. We both know she's not there yet. "When are you going to tell them about the concert?"

"I thought we could tell them over dinner." He looks at his

watch. "Hey, Harper."

"Yeah?"

"You ladies ready to eat?" he asks.

"Yes!" they shout at the same time.

"You heard the ladies," Justin says. "Let's fire up the grill and get to the main event."

"I'm not watching you have sex with your girlfriend," I say, deadpan.

"Not my girlfriend. Not yet," he says, glancing back at Harper.

"You ready to nail that down. Put a title to it?"

"I was ready the night I met her."

"Whoa, I mean, I knew you liked her, but that's some heavy shit coming from you."

"I know." He runs his hands through his hair. "It's heavy and fucking fantastic too. She's so down to earth, not at all worried about my money, or my status. When we talk about my family, it's stories of me growing up, not about the money or when she can meet them. She's one of a kind, Luke."

"That's great, man." I slap him on the shoulder. "What can I do?"

"Grab the burgers from the fridge. I'll get the grill fired up."

I head inside and gather the burgers and salt and pepper and take them back outside. "What else?"

"Just having some chips, and Harp made some potato salad this morning."

"Look at you all domesticated and shit."

He takes it as a compliment, which it was if his smile is any indication. "So when do you plan on making it official?"

"Soon. I'm trying not to scare her off, but damn, man, I'd move her in today if I thought she'd go for it."

"How do you know she won't?" I ask.

"Addyson."

"I'm not following?" Is there something going on with Addyson that I don't know about? I'm just about ready to ask him when he starts talking again.

"Her past. Harper has lived it with her. She's not as jaded as Addyson, but she's cautious. Not that I can blame her. There are a lot of assholes out there."

"Not just the male variety."

"Truth." He looks back to the pool where the girls are swimming. "I thought I loved Amy," he says quietly. "I thought she was the real deal, and even after all the shit she put me through, I missed her. Well, maybe not her, but the idea of her, of the life we were planning. Even the baby," he confesses.

He never talks about this. Amy has been locked in the vault, and he threw away the key. "And now?"

"Now, I know it wasn't real. I didn't feel for her half of what I'm already feeling for Harper. It's too soon. I know that. But damn, Luke, I can't seem to help it. It's like my heart is on a runaway train and every time I look at her, I just want to urge the conductor to go faster."

"There is no timeline," I tell him. "You feel what you feel. From the looks of it, you're not on that train by yourself."

He nods. "I just want to do it right with her. I want this to stay. I want her to stay."

"I have a good feeling, my man," I say as we watch the girls climb out of the pool. Well, my eyes are on Addyson. Water runs over her body, her dark hair looking even darker wet. I almost cry when she wraps her beach towel around her body, hiding from me. Almost. Instead, I keep my eyes glued to her as they approach us.

"What can we do?" Harper asks.

"Nothing. We're keeping it simple. You ladies grab a drink and take a seat. It won't take long for these to cook."

"Do you mind if I use your restroom?" Addyson asks.

"Sure, make yourself at home."

"I'll show you." I wait for her to walk past me and follow her inside. "Just down the hall."

"Thanks," she says, keeping her back to me.

I follow her, even though she can't see me, as she disappears behind the door. Resting my back against the wall, I wait for her. It's not lost on me that this is a first. It screams desperate, and well, maybe I am. Desperate for those brown eyes and all their attention.

When the door opens, she's startled to see me standing here like a creeper and gets her foot caught on the rug. I jump into action catching her. Her hands land on my chest, while mine circle her waist.

"Sorry about that."

I pull her close. "Never apologize for falling into my arms." Cheesy as fuck, but the words are out there, so I roll with it.

Her shoulders shake with laughter. "You never give up do you, Lucas?"

"You really want me to?" I ask her.

"I don't know," she confesses. A confession that almost sounds as if she's starting to see things my way. Maybe she finally realizes that I'm here for her. Not for what she can give me, or what she can do for me. Just her. She doesn't know if she wants me to give up? Perfect. I don't plan to.

"This…" I trace the strap of her bikini that hooks around her neck. I start at her neck and follow it to her breast, skimming lightly over the top of the material. "Drives me insane."

"This old thing?" she teases. Her tone is light, but I can tell my touch affects her by the way her breathing kicks up.

"I don't care how old it is. You look incredible in it." My index finger travels over the valley of her chest, tracing the bikini over her other breast. "Teal is my new favorite color."

"It's mine. I mean, teal, it's my favorite color."

"You make it look good."

She shakes her head in amusement. "We should probably get back out there." She says the words, but her hands are still flat against my chest.

"Yeah, no. I think I'm good right here." I give her hip a gentle squeeze.

"You're staring."

"I am."

"Why? Do I have something on my face?"

"Your lips… they look soft."

Her tongue peeks out and sweeps across her bottom lip. "So do yours."

"Yeah? Maybe we should find out?"

"Just so we don't have to wonder."

"If that's what you want to tell yourself," I say, leaning down, closing in on her. Adrenaline kicks in and pumps through my veins. I've thought of little else since the night I met her.

"One time won't hurt, right?"

I'm not sure if she's trying to convince me or herself, but I don't need convincing. "Just a taste." I close the distance slowly, my lips descending to hers. Her nails dig into my chest as a soft whimper escapes her. "Jump," I say against her lips. Tightening my grip on her hips, I lift her. Instinctively, she wraps her legs around my waist. "Better," I murmur. She's a tiny thing, and at this angle, I can kiss her. Really kiss her like I've been thinking about for weeks now.

I turn so her back is to the wall. She seems to melt into it, opening her mouth, and letting me taste her fully. My tongue touches hers for the first time, and I feel as though my senses have been short-circuited. All I feel, all I taste is her. She's intoxicating, and I know without a doubt, one kiss, this one taste will never be enough.

"Hey, you guys okay?" Harper calls. "It's time to eat."

I slow the kiss and pull away. Addyson buries her face in my neck. "Yeah, be right there," I call back. My voice is strong. Steady. However, I feel anything but.

"I don't want to let you go," I whisper. "I don't know if I'll ever get you here again, and I want to make this count."

She looks up at me. Her brown eyes swimming with desire. "You better make it count then."

Not needing to be told twice, I crush my lips to hers. This time I don't hold back. I nip at her bottom lip, taking, tasting, and memorizing her taste, her smell, the feel of her in my arms. All of it. My mind is in overdrive trying to catalogue it all. To never forget.

Her growling stomach has me pulling away. Again, she buries her face in my neck, trying to catch her breath. "Let's get you fed, sweet Addy," I whisper. She pulls away and offers me a small smile. Leaning in, I kiss the tip of her nose.

Carefully, I lower her to her feet. Her legs are wobbly, so I keep a tight grip on her until I know she can stand on her own. "I'm okay," she says, her voice husky.

Releasing her, I back away. "I need a minute," I tell her. "You can go on without me."

"What do I tell them?"

"Tell them I gave you a tour. It's believable."

"Are you —" She looks down at my dick and it twitches from the attention. "Are you gonna be okay?"

"Yeah, as soon as you stop looking at me like that."

"Right." She turns on her heel and starts to leave. She reaches out and places her hand on the wall to gain her balance. She stops walking and turns to look at me. "They're soft," she says, her eyes trailing from my dick slowly up my body until they're locked on mine. "Your lips. They're soft." She gives me a shy smile, before turning and walking away from me.

I close my eyes fighting against the urge to watch her go. That's the last thing I need to do when I'm trying to get myself under control. Counting backward from one hundred, I make it to zero and have to start over again. By the time I hit twenty for the second time, I'm able to join everyone outside.

No one asks me why it took me so long. Small favors and all that. I grab a plate and pile it up and sit next to Addyson.

chapter
eleven

Addyson

Harper and Justin are already at the table making their plates when I join them on the deck. Neither one of them asks what took us so long, or where Lucas is. They're smart. I'm sure they've figured it out.

"Help yourself, Addyson," Justin says kindly.

"Is that your potato salad?" I ask Harper. "Your mom's recipe?"

"Yep." She laughs.

"You love me," I say, piling a big spoonful on my plate.

"Sounds legendary," Justin comments.

"Oh, you have no idea. Harper's definitely got her mother's skills in the kitchen. Go ahead," I urge him. "Try it."

He takes a big fork full and moans. "Wow, this is delicious, babe." Harper beams from his praise, or maybe it's because he called her babe.

"Told you." I take a bite of my own. I hear the door open, but I ignore it and keep on eating. Lucas takes the seat next to me, his plate full.

"Man, you have to try this," Justin tells him, taking another huge bite of potato salad.

"Looks good," Lucas says. He takes a bite and nods his agreement before taking another.

Justin finishes his food in record time, sitting back in his chair. "I have a surprise," he says, and my heart stops. Surely he's not going to propose? Would he?

"Yeah?" Harper smiles over at him. She doesn't seem concerned at all.

"I might have scored four tickets to that Dan + Shay concert you were talking about."

"What?" Harper and I say at the same time.

Justin nods. "Backstage passes, meet and greet, the whole shebang." He grins like a schoolboy on picture day.

"Holy shit." Harper launches out of her chair and wraps her arms around his neck. "That's amazing. I don't even care how you did it. Wait, you didn't have to sell a kidney or anything crazy, right?" she asks him.

"No, babe. I told you, I had connections."

"EEEPP!" She crushes her mouth to his.

Looking down at my plate, I continue to eat. I can feel Lucas's eyes on me, but I refuse to look at him for fear he'll see my truth. That he'll see how much he affects me, and if I'm honest, how I'm a little jealous that I'm not kissing him right now.

I'm a mess.

I know that taking a break is the right thing to do. I need to breathe on my own, give myself time to get over the betrayal. But my body, well, it's screaming for Luke.

"You two are coming with us, right?" Harper asks, pulling

me out of my thoughts.

"Of course, they are," Justin chimes in. "That's why I got four tickets." A look passes between him and Lucas, but it's gone before I can decipher it.

"Thank you, Justin," I say.

"You're welcome. It's a date," he says, kissing Harper's bare shoulder.

Lucas coughs, and I turn to look at him. "It's a date," he mouths.

I can't resist rolling my eyes at him. If Lucas Prescott is anything, he's determined, and that twinkle in his eye is hard to resist.

***

A few hours later, we're lounging by the pool. It's been a relaxing day, and I must admit the kisses made it memorable. It's been hours, yet I can still feel his lips on mine, can still feel his hands gripping my thighs, feel him pressed against me.

"What do you ladies think about going out?" Justin asks. "I've been wanting to check out that new Escape Room downtown."

"I don't know," Harper says. "I've heard about it, but what is it exactly? They lock us in a small space, and we have to figure out how to get out?"

"Yes and no," Lucas answers. "It's a room, and you are locked in it, but there's a story to it. Kind of like a murder mystery. They give you clues that lead you to the next clue, and so on until you find the key that unlocks the door. You have an hour to escape."

"That doesn't sound too bad," Harper admits.

"So after an hour they let you out?" I ask.

"Yeah, gameplay is one hour, and if you don't escape, they unlock the door. Usually they ask to take your picture with signs saying you've been captured or something crazy. If you win, you hold up a sign saying we escaped or something similar."

I look over at Harper. "Sounds fun."

She nods her agreement. "I'd need to run home and get ready."

"Why? You look perfect as you are," Justin says. He's not blowing smoke up her ass. He looks completely confused as to why she would need to go home first.

"That would be the same for me," I tell him.

"What time does it start?" Harper asks.

"Let me look. I think you have to schedule a time to go." He grabs his phone. "Looks like we can book a four-person room at eight."

"It's just after five now, so that gives us time." Harper stands and gathers her stuff. "Addy, are you ready to go?" She eyes me and then her gaze slides to Lucas.

"Sure." I stand too, gathering my towel and the rest of my belongings. I follow Harper into the house so we can change out of our suits. When I exit the room I'm using, Lucas is standing there against the wall.

"We have to stop meeting like this," I tell him, trying to hide my smile.

"Well, that all depends on you," he says, not bothering to move from where he's leaning casually against the wall.

"Oh, yeah? How's that?"

"You ready to go out with me?"

"On a break, remember?"

"I know that's what you're telling me, but earlier, that didn't feel like a break."

"Call it an experiment."

"I call it lust. And, Addy, we have that in spades."

"I won't deny it. We're adults, Luke. We can control our hormones."

"I'm not so sure I can. My hands are still tingling from

touching your soft skin, and my lips…" He taps his lips with his index finger. "I can still taste you."

He's not alone. "I should go." I walk past him down the hall. Harper and Justin are on the deck.

"We'll pick you all up," Justin tells Harper. He looks over and sees me, and offers me a kind smile. "I'll walk you out."

I follow behind them, beach bag in hand.

"Hey, Addy," Lucas says, stopping me in my tracks.

I turn to look at him over my shoulder. Those long legs of his close the distance between us. Reaching out, he tucks my crazy chlorine-smelling, air-dried hair behind my ear. "Drive safe," he says huskily.

I swallow hard. "You too, Luke." I turn back around, and he falls into step beside me. Silently, we walk to my car.

"Let me." He reaches around me and pulls open my car door.

"Thanks." I toss my stuff into the passenger seat and climb behind the wheel. I reach for the door, but Lucas is standing there, holding it open.

"I really want to kiss you," he murmurs.

"Luke."

"I know." He gives me a slow nod. "When you're ready, you'll let me know?"

"I don't know that I'll ever be ready, Lucas."

Another nod. "I'll see you soon, Addy."

"Bye." I wave like the fumbling mess I seem to be around him and his sexy abs and deep sex-laced voice. He shuts the door closing me in. Taking a deep breath, I make it a point not to look at him as I back out of the drive and pull away.

I'm barely at the end of the street when my cell rings. I see Harper's face flash on my screen. "I just left you." I laugh.

"Spill."

"What are you talking about?" I pretend I have no clue when I know exactly what she means.

"Girl, he was looking at you like you were his last meal. What happened?"

"He kissed me. Well, we kissed, I mean."

"And?"

"And what?"

"How was it?"

How was it? Hot as hell, soft yet demanding. All-consuming. "It was good," I say instead.

"Come on, Addyson. You have to give me more than that."

"It was hot. He knows what he's doing."

"So what does it mean?"

"Nothing. We kissed. It was a moment of weakness."

"Weakness my ass. That man is hot as hell, and I see the way you look at him." She pauses. "Addyson, don't give up. What if Lucas is the one, your prince, and you never find out because you let fear guide you?"

"And what if he's like the rest of them? Look, Harp, we've had this discussion already."

"Fine. I'll just sit back and watch the story unfold. There are sure to be fireworks at the end," she says matter-of-factly.

"What's the plan?" I ask, changing the subject.

"The guys are picking us up. They'll pick me up and then we'll swing by your place. It's on the way."

"Okay. Text me when you leave your house so I can be waiting."

"Sounds like a plan. See you soon." I say goodbye and end the call.

Ten minutes later, I'm pulling into my driveway. I don't waste any time rushing inside to shower. I have a nondate date with a sexy man who makes me weak in the knees and our best friends, who are so obviously in love.

Should be a fun night.

chapter
twelve

LUCAS

I'm up to my eyeballs in paperwork for my current build. I've been putting in crazy hours this week, working with the building to get everything finalized. I'm buried in work, but that doesn't stop me from ignoring it all when my phone pings alerting me to a new text message. I texted Addyson first thing this morning telling her to have a good day. It's now after ten, and I haven't heard back, so I'm anxious. Grabbing my phone, I smile when I see her name.

Addyson: You too. It's been a busy one.

I send her a picture of my desk.

Me: I know the feeling.

Addyson: Do I need to come and dig you out?

Me: Possibly.

Me: We could have dinner after.

Addyson: I just sent Justin a text. He'll be there to pull you out of the rubble.

Addyson: Be mindful of papercuts. They're a bitch.

Me: LOL.

I toss my phone back on my desk and get back to work. There's a knock on my office door not a minute later. I don't have to look up to know it's Justin. "Did she really text you?" I chuckle.

"Yep." He steps in and takes a seat across from me. "Your desk looks just like mine," he comments. "It's been a rough week."

"Glad to know it's not just me."

"You all set for this weekend?" he asks.

"I am. I assume your girlfriend is your date?" He sent me a text late Saturday night after we all went to the Escape Room confirming their new relationship status. Thanks to the girls we escaped. They took charge and got us out of there in forty minutes.

"That she is. You still bringing your mom?"

"I am. She looks forward to this every year. Why stop a tradition? Besides, it's not like I have a girlfriend to take her place."

"She's going to be crushed when that does happen."

"Nah, she'll be so happy to see me getting serious. She'll have no problem stepping aside." My phone rings and my mom's face flashes on the screen. "Speak of the devil," I say, holding my phone up for Justin to see before answering. "Hey, Mom."

"Luke," she croaks.

"You sound awful. Are you okay?"

"Yeah, just this nasty cold. Your father and I keep passing it back and forth. I was hoping to be well by now. Honey, I don't think I can make it to the charity event tomorrow night." She coughs into the phone.

"No worries. Do you guys need anything?"

"No, dear. Better stay away so you don't get this too. We've got what we need. I'm sorry, Luke. You know I love our annual date night."

"I know you do. There's always next year," I say as she hacks up a lung in my ear. "Mom, I'll let you go. Get some rest. Call me if you guys need anything."

"Thank you. Love you," she says, and ends the call.

"She sick?" Justin asks.

"Yeah, she sounds terrible. I guess she and Dad have been passing it back and forth. She canceled for tomorrow understandably."

"So you're in need of a date?"

I shrug. "I guess so. I have no problem going alone."

"Or…" Justin smirks. "You could call Addyson."

"It's tomorrow. You think she can find a dress before then?"

"She probably has something, and if not, make it happen."

"You say that like it's so damn simple."

"That's because it is. You call her and ask her. She says yes. You inquire if she has a dress, if not, you tell her you'll cover it since she's doing you a favor."

"We are talking about the same Addyson, right? Can you really see her letting me do that?"

"No." He laughs. "But that's not the point. The point is that she knows you're willing to do whatever it takes to have her on your arm at that event tomorrow night. Play the 'Mom's always my date, and she's sick' card. She'll go."

"What would Harper think of you telling me how to manipulate her best friend?"

"She's all for it. She wants the two of you together."

"Yeah?" For some reason, hearing that her best friend approves gives me hope that one day she and I will figure this out.

"Yes, and before you ask me what she's said, I'm not telling you. I've opened my mouth and given you more than I should have. Just call her." He rises from his chair and strolls out of my office.

"What have you got to lose?" I mumble, picking up my phone. I pull up our last text.

Me: Hey, call me when you get a break in your schedule. I have a favor.

Before I can put my phone back on my desk, it's ringing. It's her. "Hey," I answer.

"Hi. You caught me at a good time. What's up?"

"Well, I'm sure Harper has told you about the charity event for our firm this weekend? The one for the American Cancer Society?"

"Yeah, she's been talking about it all week. We went dress shopping earlier this week."

"Well, how would you like to be my date?"

"It's tomorrow, Lucas. Way to give a girl some notice."

"That I'm afraid was unavoidable—" I start, but she cuts me off before I can finish.

"Nice. So your real date bailed on you so you thought you would call me, second choice. No thanks. I'm not interested. I've been second place to every single man in my life other than my father, and I refuse to be any longer," she rants before the line goes quiet.

"Addy?" I'm not sure if she's still on the line.

"I'm here. Is that all you needed? I really need to get back to work."

"Can I talk now? Please?"

She exhales loudly. "What is it, Luke?"

"I always take my mom to this event. It's become a tradition for us. She just called to tell me that she's sick. She and my dad both have bad colds, and she's not able to go." I pause, letting that sink in. "I agree with you. You should never be second best, and that's not how I see you. I didn't ask you because this is something my mom looks forward to every year, and honestly, so do I. However, if there is anyone else who I would want on my arm tomorrow night, it's you, Addyson."

"Luke, I—"

"Addyson, would you do me the honor of attending my firm's charity banquet tomorrow night? I know it's short notice, but my date, my mother, is ill, and you are the only other woman I want."

"Well, when you put it like that." She pauses. "I'm sorry, Luke. I jumped to conclusions, and it wasn't fair to you. I know I do it. It's a kneejerk reaction after all of my past relationships. I don't have much faith in men. Not anymore, unless it's my father. Well, and maybe Justin. He's turning out to be one of the good ones."

"And me?" I ask her.

"I admit, I've been quick to judge. I'm broken, Luke." I hear the defeat in her voice, and once again I'm angry at all of the fools who screwed her over. "I need some time to get myself together. I need to let the past stay in the past, but it's hard when betrayal and lies are all you know."

"Let me be the man who puts you back together. Let me be the difference between your past and your future." I don't say anymore, waiting patiently for her to work through her thoughts.

"Can we start with tomorrow night and take it from there?" Her voice is soft, uncertain.

My heart picks up speed at what this could finally mean for us. "Yes. Do you have a dress? If not, I'm happy to buy one since it's such short notice."

"That's not necessary. Just tell me what time I need to be

ready."

"I'll be at your place at six. Dinner will be served at the event."

"Okay. I'll be ready."

"Addyson?"

"Yeah?"

"I can't wait to see you."

"Me too," she whispers before the line goes dead.

I don't know how long I sit here staring at my phone. She said yes, not just to agreeing to go to the banquet with me, but… to more.

"You know, that pile of work isn't going to go away with you just staring at it," Justin says, standing in my doorway.

"Yeah." I rub my hands over my face, pulling myself out of my head.

"I'm heading out for the day. You call Addyson?"

"I did. She's in."

"Ah, that explains the staring."

"You have no idea."

"I think I do. I'm headed to Harper's. We're having dinner with her parents tonight."

"Moving right along."

"And couldn't be happier, my man. See ya tomorrow night."

"See ya."

Glancing at the clock, I see it's just past five. I'm useless here, so I pack up my laptop and head home for the weekend. I have a date to plan.

chapter
thirteen

Addyson

I left at five on the dot and headed straight to the mall. I knew that Harper and Justin were having dinner with her parents, so I called my mom for backup. I didn't give her specific information. I told her a friend needed a plus one for an event, and I needed to find a dress.

Tonight.

"Took you long enough," Mom says when I find her at the mall entrance waiting on me.

"You live like five minutes from here," I remind her.

"So, I do." She grins. "Tell me who is this friend and what kind of event are we talking about?"

"Well, he's Harper's boyfriend, Justin's, best friend. We've all hung out a few times."

"Does Harper's boyfriend's best friend have a name?" she

asks in a way only Mom can.

"Lucas."

"I like it. So why is this Lucas character waiting until the day before?"

"I assumed that as well, but I was wrong," I admit, thinking about my earlier conversation. "He takes his mom every year. It's kind of their thing. She called him earlier letting him know that she's sick and can't make it."

"Aww." She holds her hand over her heart. "This Lucas sounds like a good man. Why have you not snatched him up?" She bumps her shoulder into mine.

"I'm taking a break."

"From what?"

"Dating."

"Why on earth would you do something crazy like that? How am I ever going to become a grandmother if you take a break? You have to get back out there."

"Mom, you know all the drama that seems to follow me and relationships."

"That's not drama, Addy, that's life. It's how you move forward, how you bounce back that's important. Sure, you've dated a few tools, but you can't let that stop you."

"Like *you* know." I raised my brows at her. "You started dating Dad in high school. There just aren't any men out there who want what I want."

"What do you want?"

"I want what you and Daddy have. I want someone to come home to, someone who wants to come home to me. I want to give you those grandbabies you're always harping about. I want to know that I'm his number one."

She nods. "How do you expect to find that if you're not out there looking?"

"I don't know. I'm tired of being second best. I don't know if my heart or my ego can take another breakup."

"Life is about change, Addyson."

"I get that, Mom. I do. But look at you and Dad. No change there."

She throws her head back and laughs, causing several shoppers to glance our way. "If that's what you think, I've done you a disservice as your mother. Addy, marriage is hard work. It takes time and patience and compromise. Your father and I love each other very much, but that doesn't mean we've not had changes. Take you for example. We were first time parents, a huge change as this little angel now depended on us for everything. It was a learning curve for both of us and wasn't always storybook. Being a parent is hard, yet so rewarding, but a challenge none the less. That's just one of many examples I could throw at you. You can't let your past keep you from the future you've always dreamed of. Only you can make your dreams come true."

"I remember you telling me that in fifth grade when I was trying to win the science fair," I remind her.

"Exactly. You can't wait until the day before it's due to put together a winning project. It takes time and preparation. So does any good relationship. You have to put work into it. You have to risk pain and hurt to find love and devotion. I was lucky. I found my forever at sixteen. You, on the other hand, will be old and gray if you don't lose this 'taking a break' business."

"He's asked me out a few times," I confess.

"Let me guess. You turned him down."

"Yes. When he called me earlier, I jumped to conclusions when he said his date fell through. I kind of went off and then he calmly told me that it was his mother and then asked me in the sweetest of words to be his date."

"I knew I liked him." She smiles. "Now, let's find you a dress that will be sure to bring him to his knees."

"Do I want that?"

"I think you do. You set the pace, be the one in control. If he's in this for you, for the right reasons, he's going to have no issue with that."

"You're right. Okay. Let's do this." I let the excitement I've been trying to hide shine through my smile. I'm thrilled to be able to spend more time with Luke. Tonight is a favor, but in my fragile heart, I'm already wishing for it to be more. We go from store to store, and I start to get discouraged on being able to find something. When we walk into the final store and make our way to the formal dresses I see it. Immediately, I fall in love with it.

"That's it," Mom says when we reach the rack and I find my size, holding it up. "Go try it on."

Not needing to be told twice, I head for the dressing room. I strip down and slide into the dress easily. "Mom," I call out. "Can you come here and zip me up?"

"Oh, Addy, this is the one," she says when I turn around to face her.

I look in the mirror, turning this way and that. It's A-Line with silver mesh over the chest, near the neck, and deeper silver with dark and light teal, and soft pink beads covering the bust, and neck. The beads stop at the waistline where the long chiffon skirt in dark teal takes over.

"I love it."

"It's perfect. Do you have silver heels?" she asks.

"I do, but I want a new pair," I say, turning left to right, still admiring the dress.

"That color really brings out your tan," Mom comments. "Not to mention, it's your favorite. Do you need to tell him what color?"

"No, I don't think so. I assume he's just going black and white."

"You're probably right. Leaves more suspense for when he sees you in it. Definitely going to bring him to his knees. You look beautiful."

"Thanks, Mom. Thanks for coming with me."

"Thanks for inviting me. Your dad went to a poker game over at Fred's, so you saved me from a lonely night at home."

"Well, dinner's on me."

"After we find you some shoes." She steps out so I can get changed, and I take the dress straight to the register. After paying, we hit the shoe store next door and find an adorable pair of silver strappy heels. I find my size, try them on, and just like that, I have my outfit for tomorrow night. My palms are sweaty from my nerves and the excitement of what's yet to come.

I barely slept at all last night. I finally climbed out of bed at around seven and made some breakfast. And by that, I mean, put a bagel in the toaster. It's no fun to cook for one. I got caught up on laundry and cleaning. It's just after noon, and I still have six hours before Lucas is due to pick me up. Needing something to occupy my time, I call Harper.

"Hey, you," she answers.

"How was last night?"

"Perfect. They all hit it off so well. Justin is making plans for us to have dinner with his parents in the next couple of weeks."

"That's great, Harp. I'm so excited for you."

"How was your night?" she asks.

"Well, Mom and I went to the mall. I needed a dress."

"What for? You should have bought one while we were out on Monday."

"See, that's the thing, I didn't know I needed one."

"So are you going to tell me what it's for or do you enjoy keeping me in suspense?"

"Lucas called me yesterday just as I was getting off work."

"O-kay?"

"His date fell through for the event tonight. He asked me if I would go. I said yes."

"Wait? You said yes after he already asked someone else?" I can hear the disbelief and anger in her voice. Like me, she's assuming the worse. That's just my luck, and we both know it.

"Yes, but it's not what you think. Believe me, I told him how I felt about it. Then he proceeded to tell me who his date originally was."

"Well?" she prompts.

"His mom." I go on to tell her the story, and by the time I'm done, she's team Lucas all the way.

"He really likes you, Addyson."

"How do you know that?" It's a stupid question. Even I can tell he's into me. The more time I'm around him, the more I realize Lucas is a "what you see is what you get" kind of guy. He's not hiding an agenda. He's just Luke.

"Let's see. I've seen the way he looks at you, and Justin might have mentioned it."

"What did he say?" I'm prying, but I'm curious as to what he said. Butterflies swarm my belly just knowing that he's been talking about me to Justin.

"I'm not telling you."

"What? Why not? Come on, you have to give me something."

"No, I don't think I do. This is what needs to happen. Let it happen organically. You want to know how he feels, you need to ask him. I can tell you this. Lucas and Justin, they're the good ones. The guys you take home to meet your parents." I can hear the smile in her voice, no doubt remembering her own dinner just last night. "They're not into games."

"I didn't think the others were either."

"True, but there is something different about these two that the others didn't have."

"What's that?"

"A heart. There is no way Lucas can look at you the way he

does and be able to screw you over. Let's not forget his determination to win you over, and his promise to not break your heart. He knows your background. Hell, that's how the four of us met. He knows what he's up against, that you're fragile and broken, but he's still here. He's still standing tall waiting for you to give him the time of day."

"It's a look, Harper."

"It's a look that would have any other woman dropping her panties," she replies, making me laugh.

"He's going to be here at six. I bought a dress and shoes, and I'm nervous."

"Good. That means you're not as unaffected as you want me to believe. Want my advice?"

"Always."

"Shave everything."

"On it, boss." I chuckle.

"That's my girl. I need to go so I can start getting ready."

"Yeah, I guess since shaving everything was just added to the agenda, I should as well."

"See you in a few hours. Oh, and send me a picture of the dress."

"See you." I end the call and snap a picture of the dress lying on my bed to send to her.

Harper: OMG! Teal is your color. I can't wait to see you in it.

Me: Thanks. See you later.

Tossing my phone on the bed, I head to the shower. Time to get ready.

chapter
fourteen

LUCAS

My palms are sweating. I don't think I was this nervous for my first date when I was sixteen. Then again, that date wasn't with Addyson. Stepping up to her front door, I squeeze the flowers I bought for her tightly in one hand while lightly knocking on the door with the other.

Seconds later, she's pulling open the door, and I honest to God feel my knees go weak. Reaching out, I brace myself with my free hand against the doorframe. I'm going for casual, but I'm not so sure I'm pulling it off. "Wow," I breathe.

Her cheeks turn the slightest shade of pink. "Thank you. You look handsome."

"These are for you," I thrust the flowers at her like the fumbling fool that I am.

Just for her.

Just for Addyson.

From the moment I met her, she's been this... light. I can't describe it really. It's as if she calls to me on a deeper level.

"Thanks, come on in, and I'll put them in some water." She steps back, letting me pass before closing the door.

I don't take my eyes off her as she fills a vase she finds under the sink and puts the flowers in water. "Ready," she says, looking up at me.

"Yes, but first I need to show you something. We match," I tell her, tugging up the leg of my suit to show her my teal socks.

"How did you know I'd be wearing teal?"

I shrug. "I didn't. I know it's your favorite, and my favorite on you. I thought worse-case scenario you would know that I was thinking about you when I got ready."

"You're one of a kind, Lucas Prescott."

"Come here." I hold my hand out for her. She doesn't hesitate as she moves toward me and places her hand in mine. "Can I just look at you for a minute?" I rake my eyes over her. "Jesus, Addyson, you're stunning."

"I already agreed to go out with you tonight. No need for flattery."

"It's the truth. You take my breath away." I wish just once she would believe me when I tell her how beautiful she is. I wish she would believe me when I tell her she's the only woman I want. Then, when I tell her that I'm falling in love with her, she'll believe me too.

"Lucas Prescott, who knew you had a silver tongue?"

"Thank you," I say, my tone serious. "For coming with me tonight. You took a lot of pressure off my mom. She's already called twice asking me to thank you for her. Oh, and she wants to meet you."

"Well, tell her it was my pleasure." She hesitates then says, "I'd love to meet her."

I nod and hold my arm out for her. It's a small victory, one I'm not going to make a big deal out of, even though inside I'm celebrating. Addy doesn't need the validation. She knows what she's just agreed to. "Ready?" Her answer is to slide her arm through mine. "You have what you need?" I ask. She points to a little silver purse sitting on the table by the door. She picks it up on our way out, and I watch as she makes sure her door is locked before guiding her to my car.

"What happened to the truck?" she asks.

"It's at home. I thought the car was more fitting for tonight. I wasn't sure, but I assumed climbing into my truck in a dress and heels is not exactly a good time."

"You guessed right." She grins. "Nice ride."

"Thank you." I open the door for her then wait for her to be settled and buckled in before shutting it. It's the gentlemanly thing to do, but honestly, it was hard to pull my eyes off her. I'm one lucky bastard to have her on my arm tonight.

I keep glancing over at her every chance I get. When she places her hand on my arm, I turn to look at her once again.

"You okay?" she questions.

"No." I signal and pull into a grocery store parking lot. We're maybe a mile from the venue, but this can't wait.

"What's wrong?" Addyson asks, concerned.

"This." Sliding my hand behind her neck, I pull her close, and I have every intention of kissing her, but stop just before our lips touch and rest my forehead against hers. My breathing is accelerated, as is hers. Her soft breaths brush against my skin. "I want to kiss you so fucking bad right now," I whisper.

"Why did you stop?" she asks breathlessly.

"Makeup. You took the time to get all dolled up, and I'm not messing that up by mauling you in my car before we even get to the event."

"Makes sense," she says, defeated.

"I want to though," I say, pulling away and staring into her eyes. "You deserve better than that, and I'm going to give it to you, but..." I trace the column of her neck with my thumb. "Once this event is over. When I take you home at the end of the night, these lips are mine," I say huskily.

"Promise?"

It takes a minute for her words to register. My heart thumps heavily in my chest. This is one promise I intend to keep. *On my life.* "Promise." I place a kiss on her cheek.

When we arrive at the event, I take advantage of the valet parking, tossing the attendant my keys. I don't warn him to take it easy. I don't give him a look telling him not to fuck up my ride. I barely spare him a glance before placing my arm around Addyson's waist and guiding her into the building.

"Wow." She takes in the room before her. "This is... not what I expected."

"What did you expect?"

"Honestly, I'm not sure, but this wasn't it. It's super fancy. I feel completely out of place."

Leaning in so only she can hear me, I say. "Take a good look around, Addy. Really look. Every man in this room has his eyes on you."

She looks up at me. "Funny, the only man I notice is you."

Warmth floods my chest at her words. Finally. I pull her closer and kiss her forehead. It's not what I want, but it will have to do for now. Until I can get her alone and kiss the hell out of her. "Come on, you. Let's go find Justin and Harper."

It doesn't take long for us to find them standing on the opposite side of the room. "Addyson." Harper pulls her from my arms and into a hug. "Girl, you look hot," she says, releasing her and motioning with her hands for her to turn in a circle. Addyson obliges, even striking a pose.

"Your turn," Addyson says, doing the same to Harper who hams it up just as much.

"Didn't think you were going to make it," Justin says from

beside me.

"Yeah, traffic," I lie.

"Justin, will you take a picture of us?" Harper asks, pulling her phone out of her small purse.

"Mine too," Addyson says, handing me her phone.

We take a few shots and then trade off. They take some of us and we take some of them. I'm already making a mental note to have one of the many they took of us printed and framed. I'm not much on pictures, not really, but this one is different. Addyson is different.

"You send your mom a picture?" She'd told me in the car on the way over that her mom helped her pick out the dress. I slide my phone back in my pocket waiting for her answer. The last thing I want to do is stand here staring at my phone all night, not when I finally got her to agree to go out with me. This is our first official date. Anything that's not Addyson can wait.

"No, but I will." She pulls her phone back out of her purse and types out a message. She smiles and turns the screen to me.

Mom: Handsome! When can I meet him?

"Sounds like our mothers are one and the same."

"She's cheering for you. For us, I guess," she says, placing her phone back in her purse. She seems to be very interested in her shoes. I know it's her confession that has her eyes on anything but me.

I wait for her to look at me. "That means you talked about me? About us?" I don't bother trying to hide my grin.

She shrugs. "A little."

I slide my arm around her waist and move in close to her. "Good." I drop a kiss to her temple, letting my actions speak for me.

I feel her body relax against me. "So what's the deal? How's this night supposed to go?" she questions, changing the subject.

"This is cocktail hour," I explain. "It gives everyone time to arrive and look at the auction items. It's a silent auction. Then we take our seats for dinner. The owner of my firm, Robert, makes a speech. Then there's dessert, more drinks, dancing, and then we go home."

"So they're raising money for the American Cancer Society?"

"Yeah, Robert lost both of his parents to cancer. This charity is close to him. He and his wife started this event about fifteen years ago. It gets bigger and better every year."

"And you've always brought your mom?"

"Yep. I was an intern in my first year and didn't want to risk bringing a date who could potentially ruin things for me. You never know how people are going to act once they get around people with money and alcohol. Anyway, I asked Mom to go, and she was thrilled. We've made it our tradition."

"That's sweet of you."

"Shh, don't tell anyone. I don't need word getting out. I'm kind of trying to impress this girl, and well, I don't need anyone in my way."

"Must be some girl." She shakes her head with a smile playing on her lips.

"You are." I hold her stare, causing her to blush.

"Let's go check out the auction." She steps away but grabs my hand and leads me to the row of tables filled with items. I don't hide my grin. She reached for me. This time it's she who's dragging me away, and I couldn't be happier. This night has been good for us. For the first time, deep in my gut, I feel like there is an us.

The night rolls on, and it feels like time is flying by. I'm usually watching the clock, waiting for a respectable time to leave. Tonight, I'm still watching the clock, but it's with the hope that time is slowing down. I'm not ready for my time with her to end. Justin and Harper are seated at our table, as well as Robert and his wife, Cecelia, and their two daughters, and their husbands. The food is great, and the company even better.

Once the dinner plates are taken away and the dessert carts have been wheeled around, the music is turned up and the dancing begins. "Dance with me," I whisper in her ear.

"You asking?" She raises an eyebrow.

"I'm telling you that I need my body aligned with yours on that dance floor. I can't be held responsible for my actions if I have to wait a minute longer," I counter.

Cecelia leans over and whispers, "Honey, you better get out there."

"Lucas!" Addy's eyes widen.

I shrug. "I'm not ashamed," I say, pushing back from the table, standing and offering her my hand.

"He's a good one," Cecelia says, not bothering to lower her voice.

"He has his moments." Addy places her hand in mine and lets me help her to her feet. We reach the dance floor and I pull her into my arms. Her hands rest just behind my neck as we sway to the beat.

"Thank you for this, for tonight. I've had a great time." Her cheeks are still a slight shade of red from her earlier embarrassment, or should I say amusement. Her smile was as wide as her eyes when she scolded me.

"Me too," I say, pulling her just a little closer. "This dress..." I shake my head. "I meant it when I told you that you took my breath away."

"I'm learning that about you," she says softly, almost to herself.

We dance for three slow songs in a row before taking a break to grab something to drink. We settle back at the table.

"You bid on any items?" Justin asks.

"Nah, just wrote a check." I do that every year. Let the others fight over the items. I don't need something in return to donate to a good cause.

"Me too. We're heading out," he tells me as he and Harper stand from their seats. I watch as Harper and Addyson say goodbye with a quick hug.

"What about you? You ready to head home?" I ask her.

"I think so. I didn't sleep well last night," she says, covering her mouth in a yawn.

Pulling out her chair, we say our goodbyes and head outside. I give the valet my tag to pull my car around.

"It's a nice night." Addyson tilts her head back to look at the stars.

"It is," I agree as my car pulls up in front of us. The valet opens the door for her, but I wave him off, waiting for her to be settled before I shut it. The ride to her place is filled with conversation. We both like all kinds of music, we both love pasta of any kind, and her middle name is Grace.

"What's yours?" she asks as I pull into her drive.

"Oliver, after my dad. It was his dad's name, and it's his middle name. And then there's my nephew, Ollie."

"Family name. I like it."

"Stay put," I tell her before climbing out of the car and jogging to her side. I open her door and offer her my hand. With her hand held tightly in mine, I walk her to her door. "Thank you for tonight." I pull her close, unable to resist putting my hands on her.

"It was fun. Thanks for having me. I'm sure your mom is sad she missed it."

"Meh, she was fine once she found out you were going with me." I'm downplaying it a little. To say that my mom's excited is an understatement.

"There's always next year, right?" She chuckles.

"You volunteering?" I ask her. The thought of her being on my arm again next year and the year after that is more than appealing. I've never looked that far ahead in a relationship, but with Addy, looking ahead is all I can seem to do.

"I-I meant for your mom."

"Maybe." I shrug. "Depends on if I can convince you to go again." The more I think about it, the more I like the idea. Love it in fact.

"That's a year away, Lucas."

"I know. Now, I think I have a promise to keep."

"That's a tall order to fill."

"You think so? Here I was thinking it will be the easiest promise I've ever made."

Her hands go to my suit jacket and she pretends to be smoothing it out. I cover her hands with mine, where they now rest over my heart. "You feel that?"

"Your heart," she answers.

"Can you feel it?" She nods. "You do that. You make my heart race. Every time I'm with you I feel as though it could beat right out of my chest. So yes, Addyson, it's a tall order, a promise made for the future. But this…" I tap my hand over hers. "…this steady rhythm is all for you."

"You're making this hard on me." She smiles up at me.

"How so?"

"I don't know how much longer I can resist you."

"Then don't." Cupping her cheek in my hand, I slowly lean in, giving her time to stop me. She doesn't. Instead, those brown eyes of hers sparkle in the moonlight. Closing the distance, I press my lips to hers. Softly, slowly, I kiss her. I have to remind myself this is a first-date goodnight kiss, not a "get the door open so I can fuck you against it" kiss. Those will come later. Right now, I need to take this slow. Show her who I am and that all I want is her.

Slowing the kiss, I eventually pull back, tracing her bottom lip with my thumb. "Goodnight, Addy." Her hands grip my suit jacket.

"Night, Luke." She slowly opens her fingers and releases me from her iron grip. Part of me wishes she would pull me inside with her, and from the look in her eyes, I'd bet money that she wants that too. However, it's too soon for her, and we both know that. No matter how much attraction is there, she has to be ready for it. I'm ready and waiting when that time comes.

Stepping back, I let my hand fall from her face. I wait for her to unlock her door, and slip inside. When I hear the lock click on the door, I turn and walk away.

chapter
fifteen

Addyson

It's been two weeks since the banquet, and Luke and I have fallen into a pattern of sorts. He texts me every day all day. We have dinner a couple of nights a week, and last weekend, we ended up at Stagger on a double date with Harper and Justin. It was a night of laughing and cutting up. The more time our little group spends together, the more obvious it becomes. Fate stepped in and brought these men into our lives, and we're both better because of it. His persistence wore me down and I'm no longer fighting against him. Instead, I'm prying open my closed-off heart and hoping that when he fully slips his way inside, he'll want to stay there.

It's Saturday night, and Luke has declared it date night. He won't tell me where we're going, but he did say it was country. I asked him what I should wear, and he told me to dress as I would for a concert, one that's indoors this time of year. I'm pretty sure we're not going to a concert since we are going to see Dan + Shay with Harper and Justin soon. I've tried to pull it out of him all week, but he's not budging. He says he wants to surprise me. I don't hate the idea; it's one I'm not used to that's for sure. None of the men in my past ever tried to surprise me with anything, date or otherwise. Well, that is unless you count their wives, girlfriends, or the fact that they were batting for the other team.

So, here I am standing in front of the full-length mirror in my room, questioning my outfit. I decided on a cream-colored sundress, with a thick brown belt around my waist. I'm wearing my brown cowboy boots with teal stitching, and my hair is down with lots of loose curls. I turn side to side making sure everything is in place, second-guessing my selection when there's a knock at the door. That has to be Luke. He's fifteen minutes early, something I've come to learn about him. He's always early. He hates to be late for anything.

"Addy," he all but growls when I open the door. He steps into me, slides his hand behind my neck, and draws me into a kiss. Despite the growl, this kiss is slow and sweet, and he's pulling away way too soon for my liking. That's something else I've learned about Luke, kissing him… it's a life-altering experience. It's as if with a simple touch of his lips, he's erasing everything from the past. The men who cheated, lied, and the ones who used me. It's more than just his kiss, it's the emotion behind it. The way he holds me, tender yet strong. The way he growls my name, not from anger but from hunger. Hunger for me.

"Hey." I'm breathless as he pulls away from the kiss.

"You look incredible."

"Thanks. You're looking pretty good yourself." I pat his chest and take a step back, putting some much-needed distance between our heated bodies. Also, I need to get a good look at him. He's wearing faded jeans, which cling tightly to his thighs. There's a rip in the knee, and I can't tell if it's from use or if he bought them that way. Regardless, he looks hot. He's wearing a tight-fitting T-shirt. It's solid black, and it does nothing to hide the ridges and planes of his muscles.

"Unless you want me to cancel our plans, you're gonna need to stop looking at me like that."

I take my time, making my way up his body until our eyes meet. "Would that be so bad?" It's the first time I've said something so bold to him about us.

"No," he chokes out the word. "But it's not going to happen. I'm wooing you."

"Wooing me?" I laugh, stepping back so he can enter my condo.

"Yes. You're still skittish. Until you're not, until you know I'm in this with you, it's only goodnight kisses." He taps my nose with his index finger.

His words light up my shaded heart. It's hard for me to trust in this, in him after everything, but he's given me no reason not to. He shouldn't be punished for my past. But taking it slowly, that's exactly what I need, and he somehow understands that. Not only does he understand it, but he's also embracing it.

"And hello kisses." I grin.

"Yeah, and maybe some in-between kisses." He leans in and kisses the corner of my mouth. "You ready?"

I look down at my outfit. "Does this work for where we're going?"

"How do you know it's not a concert?" he teases. I give him a look that tells him we both know he's full of shit. "Fine." He chuckles. "Yes, it's perfect. You're perfect," he adds.

"Let me grab my purse." I rush to the living room and snag my small crossbody bag from the couch. I double check I have my small wallet, phone, and keys before following him out to his truck.

***

"What?" I try to sit up in my seat, but the seat belt prevents me from doing so. "Is this what we're doing?"

"Yep."

"This is awesome." I take in the huge sign advertising the rodeo.

"Yeah?"

"Definitely. I've never been."

"I wasn't sure, but it reminded me of that night at the festival. I thought it would be fun."

"Thank you. I'm excited."

"Me too. I know you said you had a late lunch, so I thought we could snack here and grab something after?" he suggests.

"That's perfect." As soon as the truck is in park, I'm hopping out and bouncing on the balls of my feet waiting for him to join me. When he finally reaches the front of the truck, I grab his hand and lead us through the crowd. Tickets scanned, cold draft beer in hand, we head to our seats. "Holy shit, Luke. We're front row." I turn to look at him over my shoulder.

He shrugs. "I wanted you to really experience it."

If we weren't standing in the middle of a crowd, and I wouldn't spill my beer, I'd jump in his arms and kiss him. Turning back around, I take each step one at a time as we near the first row where our seats are. Just as I'm getting ready to sit, I hear a female voice yell out Lucas at the top of her lungs. Stopping, I turn to see a cute little blonde and a gaggle of her friends approach the end of our row.

"Lucas." She tries for sexy, but it comes out all whiney. "I haven't seen you in forever." She lays her hand on his arm.

Anger bubbles up inside me, maybe a little humiliation too. It all quickly fades as I watch him jerk his arm from her hold. He turns to face me, holding out his hand. I step into him instead, and he wraps his arms around me. "Kelsey." His tone is even. "Meet my girlfriend, Addyson. Baby, this is Kelsey. We went to high school together."

Flutters in my belly replace my anger. I'm not quite sure if it's because he clearly dismissed her for me, called me his girlfriend, or because he called me baby. I'm going to go with all three. Lucas Prescott is a storm that rolled into my life, slow and steady, making himself known. No matter how much I try to guard my heart, he breaks down the barriers, one at a time. I'm falling for him, and that scares me to death. I don't know if I would ever be able to come back from losing him.

He's... more.

He's everything.

"Nice to meet you." Instead of offering her my hand, I make a show of resting it on Lucas's chest. Her eyes flare just for a moment before it's masked.

"You too."

"I didn't know you were seeing someone."

"Why would you?" he asks her.

She flinches as if he slapped her. "Well, when you're free, call me."

"Don't hold your breath," he tells her before he looks down at me. I know this because I turned away from her and glued my eyes to him. "We're going the distance." His voice is loud, firm, but his eyes, they're soft, and all for me. Bending, he kisses me on the forehead. "It was good to see you." He tells them, then turns us and guides me down the row to our seats.

My heart pounds against my chest. I know I should say something, maybe tell him he didn't have to be so short with her, but I can't seem to form the words. Instead of feeling sorry for her, I'm elated for me.

He chose me.

Placing my beer in the cup holder in front of us, I turn to him. Reaching out, I run my hand along the week-long beard. "Can I kiss you, Luke?" I ask softly.

He leans in close. "Every day for the rest of your life." He doesn't give me a chance as he presses his lips to mine. Just a quick peck, but the sentiment is there. Pulling away, he laces his fingers through mine, and we settle in to watch the rodeo.

Looking around, there are way more women here than men, and from the conversation from the rowdy group behind us, they're here for the riders. That's fine by me. The only man who has my attention is sitting next to me.

"You like Wrangler butts?" he whispers in my ear, causing me to laugh.

"Meh, they're not bad," I tease.

"Not bad, huh? What does it for you, Addyson?" He's joking, but his facial expression is anything but.

"You're wearing Rock's, right?"

"Yeah, Rock Revival."

"That'll work."

He throws his head back in laughter and places his arm around my shoulders. That's how we sit throughout the last hour of the show.

"Ladies and gentlemen, if you could remain seated. We have special guest Eric Ethridge here tonight," the announcer says once the final bull has been ridden and the last barrel has been raced.

"Did you know about this?" I ask Luke.

"Yeah, I knew someone was going to be here, but I didn't look into it. I'd never heard of him. I just wanted you to see the bull riding."

"You want to stay?"

"That's your call. I'm good either way."

"Let's stay for a song or two?" I suggest, watching as the crowd thins. Mostly those with small kids.

"Fine by me. You need another beer or anything?"

"No, I'm good. Thank you," I say, just as the lights begin to dim. The remaining crowd climb to their feet, as do we. His hands move to my hips, and then the heat of his body aligns with mine. He wraps his arms around my waist, and without hesitation, I relax into him.

Eric Ethridge begins to play "If You Met Me First." It's not exactly us, but it's pretty damn close. It fits us. If I had met Luke prior to all the others before him, I can't help but think that things would have been different. Maybe I wouldn't have pushed him away. His hold tightens, and unable to control it, I turn and wrap my arms around him. We slowly sway to the music, letting the lyrics speak for us.

"Maybe you still can," Lucas whispers in my ear as the song ends. He doesn't say it, but I know he's referring to the song.

I look up at him. The room is dark, but I can see the intensity in his eyes. Standing on tiptoes, I place my lips next to his ear. He bends to help me, his hands on my hips. "I want to," I confess. "Just give me some time."

His reply is to crush me in a hug with his strong arms. It rivals every hug I've ever received. "You ready?" he asks before pulling away.

"Yes." With my hand held tightly in his, he leads up the stairs, out of the arena, and to his truck.

chapter
sixteen

LUCAS

As we walk out of the arena hand in hand, I feel as though we've made a giant step forward tonight. I'd never heard of that artist, but that song, although not our exact situation, the sentiment is perfect for us.

I want to.

Her whispered confession has me smiling wide. I've fallen for her. Not just, hey I like this girl, but hey, I can see my future with her. We're on the right track, and I can give her all the time she needs.

"You hungry?" I ask once we're both settled in my truck.

"I am."

"What sounds good?"

"We could just grab a pizza or something and take it back to my place."

Although the idea is appealing, there is one that appeals to me more. "How about we take it to mine? I'd like you to see my place."

"Sure," she agrees easily. No hesitation. I love this new side of us. I can only hope we keep moving in this direction.

She calls in our order for pizza and boneless wings, and by the time we get to the mom-and-pop place just down from my house, our order is ready. When we pull into my driveway, she gasps.

"Luke, this is your place?" Astonishment fills her voice.

My chest fills with pride. I designed this place. "Home sweet home," I tell her.

"I love this house. I've driven by here hundreds of times. This is my dream home." She stares out the window into the night. I have floodlights on the house, lighting it up.

Something else, something I can't explain mixed with the pride I was feeling earlier warms my chest. "Well," I say, parking in the garage. I made sure there was an attached bay large enough for my truck. "Let me give you the tour."

Room by room, I walk her through my house. She's quiet as she just takes it all in. We start upstairs. There are four bedrooms, two full bathrooms, and an open entertainment area that looks out over the living room. "This is huge," she comments.

"It's my forever home."

"Definitely," she agrees, following me back downstairs.

Again, I take her through each room. She stops in the kitchen, her mouth hanging open. "Holy cow, this is huge."

"You cook?" I ask.

"No. Well, I mean, yes, I can. I know how." She fumbles for her words as she runs her hand over the granite countertop. "I just don't do it often. Not much fun to cook for one, but if I had a kitchen like this, I'd probably cook big meals every night. I'd be as big as this house." She laughs.

"Well, my kitchen is open to you anytime."

"You cook?"

"I do. Mom taught me and my sister, Anna. Said she wanted us both to be independent."

"My mom was always in the kitchen when I was growing up. I loved watching her. She made it all look so effortless."

"We should cook together," I suggest.

"Yeah. We should." She grins. "It's beautiful, Lucas. You should be proud."

"There's one more room." I point to the hallway off the kitchen. Her eyes light up. "Go on back. The door is at the end of the hallway."

She doesn't hesitate. I follow behind her, wanting to see her reaction.

"Wow," she whispers.

"This is my room," I say, sneaking up behind her. She doesn't move a muscle as she takes in my room, maybe my stealth skills are not as good as I thought they were. She turns in a circle taking it all in. I try to see it through her eyes. Black king California four-poster bed, black nightstands nestled on either side, black dressers, gray walls, with a gray, black, and white striped comforter set. It's very masculine, as it should be since it's just me.

"This is you." She turns to face me. "It suits you."

"You haven't even seen the best part." I reach for her hand and lead her to the bathroom.

"This is huge." She pulls her hand from mine to explore. "This shower is big enough for ten people," she comments.

"A man has to have room."

"What exactly are you doing in this shower, Lucas?" she asks, then immediately holds up her hand. "Forget I asked. I don't want to know."

I grin. "Just showering," I assure her. "There have only been two other women in this room other than you."

"Oh."

"Damn it, that's not how it was supposed to sound. My mom and my sister, Addy.

They're the only women who have ever been to this house."

She nods, but I'm not so sure she believes me. When she turns, she rushes to the

clawfoot tub. "This is awesome, and I've never seen one this huge before. You take a lot of baths, do you?"

"No, I've actually never used it."

"Then why have it?" She tilts her head to the side, studying me.

"My wife."

I see her face instantly pale.

"No," I rush to say.

Fuck!

"Addy, no, that's not what I meant. I meant my *future* wife." I could seriously smack myself. "Come here, look." I clamp my hand around hers and lead her out of the bathroom and to the two walk-in closets. "This one's mine," I tell her. I make sure she gets a good look, then lead her to the other door. I push it open and flick on the light. The shelves are bare. I keep fucking this up. I can see she's closing off on me and I can't have that.

I pull her into my arms, her back to my chest so she can see the empty room. "I'm a planner, Addyson. I plan every detail of homes and buildings, and that flows over into my life. I wanted my dream home, my forever home. I also want to marry someday, have a couple of kids. I needed to know that my family could grow into this house, that when I finally find the woman I want to spend the rest of my life with, she would have everything she needs."

"Okay," she whispers.

"Addyson." I turn her in my arms and cup her face in the

palm of my hands. "I swear to you. You can call my mother and ask her. Hell, call my sister. Anna would be thrilled to tell you all of my shortcomings, but I can promise you being married isn't one of them."

"Are you hiding anything? Engagements, weddings, kids?" she rattles off, her voice flat.

"No, baby," I say softly. "None of that. Never been close to being engaged or married. I don't have any kids, but I want all of that."

Her eyes stare into mine, the brown orbs wavering on trusting me. Not leaving anything to chance, I pull my phone out of my pocket and dial my mom. "Hey, Mom," I greet her when she answers.

"Luke, I thought you were on a date."

"I was, I mean, I am. Addy loved it just like I thought she would."

"That's great, dear."

"Mom, I need a favor?" Addy tries to pull away, already shaking her head, but I hold tightly. "You see, I keep putting my foot in my mouth with her, and well, I need her to ask you a question, and I want you to answer her. Can you do that?"

"Of course. Luke, is everything okay?" I'm sure she detects the desperation in my voice.

"It will be," I assure her. I hand the phone to Addyson. "Ask her."

"No. Lucas, this is crazy."

"No. It's not crazy. I keep fucking up." I hear my mom scold my language, but I push through. "I need you to be able to trust me, Addyson. Please, just take the phone and ask her."

She nods. She needs this. "H-hello," she says into the phone. I keep my arms around her waist, holding her close. "Hi." Her face blushes. "It's nice to talk to you as well. Luke talks about his family all the time." I can hear my mom tell her that she's heard a lot about her, which is an understatement. Addyson is all I think about and talk about these days. "I'm sorry he's bothering you with this," she tells my mom. I can't hear her reply, but Addyson smiles. "Yeah, so we uh, we were talking and —"

"Just ask her, Addy," I whisper.

"Has Luke, I mean, Lucas, has he ever been married or engaged? Does he have any kids?" she rushes to ask. "Not that any of that matters to me, but I've not had the best of experiences with men and lying and I just… I would just like to know the truth up front," she sighs, sounding almost defeated, and I hate it.

I can't make out what my mom is saying, but I can feel Addyson's body relax against me. I kiss the top of her head. I just hope this doesn't push us back when just a few hours earlier, I felt as though we were finally moving forward.

"Thank you, Mrs. Prescott." I assume my mom scolds her for that when Addyson says, "Gail." She listens then says, "That would be nice. Just have Lucas let me know." Another pause. "Thank you, you too." Addyson hands the phone up to me.

"Hey, Mom."

"Luke, she sounds lovely."

I smile down at Addyson. "She's more than lovely, Mom. She's the difference." I wink at Addyson, and she rolls her eyes, which tells me she gets my reference. Not only do I want to be that for her, but she's also that for me. I may not have had all the drama she's had in relationships, but I haven't found the one. Well, until now. I'm sure the woman in my arms is the only one I'll ever want forever. I promise Mom I'll call her later this week, and end the call.

"Our pizza is probably cold." I kiss Addyson's forehead and lead her back out to the kitchen. Surprisingly, the pizza is still warm. We fill our plates, grab two bottles of water, and settle in the living room.

"I'm sorry," she says once we're seated. "I know I'm acting crazy, and calling your mom…" She shakes her head. "I'm embarrassed."

I reach out and place my hand on her knee. "I know you've had a hard time. Hell, that's how I met you that night. I heard you talking about it. You have nothing to be embarrassed about. My mom, damn, my entire family knows about you. I have nothing to hide from anyone. If a phone call to my mother helps you work through your fears, then we can call her as many times as you want."

"It's so hard for me to trust, and that's not fair to you, Luke. I know that. I'm being unreasonable and what's worse is I don't know how to stop it."

"You don't. Time will. You let me show you I'm not any of those bastards from your past." I pause then decide to go for it. I'm all-in with her. "I'm your future, Addyson."

She nods, her eyes glassy with tears. "Thank you for being patient with me."

"We have a lifetime," I tell her. "Now eat. It's really going to be cold."

After we've finished eating, we head out to the deck.

"Wow, the outside is just as stunning as the inside," she says, looking over the three-tier deck at the hot tub and the pool.

"Thank you. There are some lounge chairs over here." I point to the corner of the top level we're on. I settle on one of the larger chaises and pat the spot next to me. "Sit with me."

To my relief, she doesn't hesitate to sit, pull off her boots, and curl up against my chest. "This is nice."

"It is. I'm glad you're here, Addy. In my home, in my space. I've pictured you here a thousand times, but you being here, sharing a place that's so special to me with you is better than I could have imagined it to be." We let the quiet of the night surround us, just happy to be here in this moment with one another. Time passes and when she starts to yawn, I know it's time to take her home. Except I don't want to. I want her here. With me.

"Sleepy?" I ask.

"Yeah, it's been a long day."

"I can take you home if you're ready." I pause. "Or you could stay. Here. With me." She's quiet, and I start to worry I said the wrong thing for the third time tonight.

"When you say with you...?" she questions.

I don't need her to say it. She's not ready for more, and I'm okay with that. "I mean, you and me, just like this in my bed. I want to hold you."

More silence.

Nothing but the silence of night surrounds us.

"Okay."

Her softly spoken words reach in and touch my soul. She stands, gathers her boots, and waits for me to join her. Hand in hand, we head back inside the house. I take her with me as I lock all the doors and turn off the lights. In my room, I pull my T-shirt out of my drawer and hand it to her. "You can sleep in this."

"Thanks." She disappears into my monster of a bathroom all on her own. I strip out of my jeans and T-shirt, leaving on my boxer briefs. I turn off the overhead light and switch on the one on the nightstand.

The door opens, and she walks out. Face scrubbed free of the little makeup she wore, she looks stunning, especially wearing my shirt. "I-I wasn't sure if you have a favorite side of the bed," I say, trying not to toss her on the bed and make love to her. She's a fucking vision standing before me.

"No preference." She surprises me when she walks to the left side of the bed, the opposite side of where I'm standing, pulls back the covers, and climbs in.

I do the same and then turn off the lamp. She moves to the

middle of the bed, and I meet her halfway, holding my arms open for her. It takes her a few minutes, but she eventually relaxes. "Night, Luke." She yawns.

"Night, Addy." I kiss the top of her head and close my eyes. I fall asleep quickly with her tucked safely in my arms.

chapter
seventeen

Addyson

My eyes blink open and then close tightly, blocking out the bright sun shining through the window. Lifting my hand to block the light, a deep chuckle wraps around me like an embrace.

"I've been fighting that sun for the last hour," Lucas's deep voice declares from behind me.

I roll over in his arms. "Why didn't you get up and close it? I could still be sleeping." I poke him in the chest.

"Two reasons. One, I told you I would hold you all night, and I'm a man of my word. Two, I don't know if this is a one-time thing. I don't know how long until I get to lie with you beside me like this again, so I'm soaking up every ounce of you I can while it's here and available."

I can feel embarrassment flush my cheeks. I should tell him

there will be more mornings like this. I should tell him he's broken through my walls, and I'm falling for him. Instead, I keep it light and playful. "You're a sweet talker in the morning light."

"Nah, that's just me, Addy. The me that is falling so fucking hard for you." He reaches out and smooths what I'm sure is my crazy bedhead hair out of my eyes. "I know it's soon, but I'm falling, Addyson. I want to make that known. I don't play games and have no intention of starting now." My heart trips over in my chest at his confession. I want to believe him, and on some level, I do. I'm still just hesitant. I have a feeling losing Lucas would rival any prior pain my heart has endured.

"I really like you," I confess. My heart is beating so loud I'm sure he can hear it. To be honest, I more than really like him, but telling him makes me vulnerable. It opens me up for pain and heartache. It gives this... whatever it is we're doing the ability to crush me if it doesn't work out.

"Good." He kisses my forehead, and I snuggle into his chest. "As long as we're both heading in that direction. What are your plans for today?"

His change of subject shows he already knows me so well. It's both scary and exhilarating. "Laundry, I'm so far behind. And I need to go to the grocery store. You?"

"I could go to the store, and I have some work to do."

I sit up, taking that as my cue to go, but he pulls me back to the bed. "What are you doing?"

"Getting dressed, getting out of your hair."

"Did I tell you that you were in my hair? That I wanted you to leave?"

"No."

"Exactly. Now, I say we go make some breakfast together in my big-ass kitchen, then we go to the store for both of us. We can drop my stuff off then head to your place. I can work on what I need to, and you can get caught up on your laundry."

I let his words sink in. "Really? You just want to... grocery shop and hang out while I do laundry?"

"I have work to do," he reminds me.

"Yeah, but—" I stop collecting my thoughts. "I've never had that. Usually, it's 'have a good day.' And, I've never cooked with a guy before."

"Those other men were douchebags. I want all your minutes, all your hours, all your days. So, yes, Addy. I want to make breakfast with you. I want to go grocery shopping, and then I want to sit on your comfortable couch with my laptop, with you beside me in between loads of laundry."

I can't hide my smile. "Sounds like the perfect day."

His lips brush the top of my head. "You want to take a shower?"

"Uh, I can wait, but do you maybe have some shorts or sweats that I can wear home? And we're going to have to stop there before we go to the store."

"That's fine." He shrugs. "That's more time with you." He lightly taps my ass with his big hands and climbs out of bed. I take in his chiseled abs, and... my eyes widen when I see his erection in his boxer briefs that leaves nothing to the imagination.

"Addy," he growls.

My eyes snap up. "Huh?"

"I said..." He takes a deep breath. "If you keep looking at me like that, we won't leave this room."

Yes, please. "Oh, sorry, I just...." I nod to his obvious erection.

"That's all for you, beautiful. You can't expect me to sleep with you curled up in my arms and not be affected."

"But... doesn't it hurt?" I blurt.

"I'm fine," he assures me. "As long as you stop looking at me like that."

I close my eyes. "Okay. You should maybe just... um, get

dressed and let me know when I can open."

"You don't have to close your eyes, Addyson."

"No, really I do. I can't stop looking, and I know we're not there yet, but I mean, I'm not so sure it's going to fit." I bite my lip to keep more embarrassing word vomit from spewing out. I can hear him moving around the room. It's not until I feel his hot breath against my neck that I know he's close.

He places a soft kiss on my neck, just below my ear. "I'll fit, baby," he assures me. "When the time is right, when you trust me enough to make it good for you, for both of us. I promise you, I'll fit." One more sweet kiss, and I feel him pull away. "You can open your eyes, Addy."

I hesitate, then slowly open my eyes to find him standing before me. He's in gym shorts, a T-shirt, and a backward hat. "I left some sweats on the bed. You'll have to roll them up. They're going to swallow you, but they'll work to get us to your place."

"Thank you, Luke."

He nods, turns, and walks out of his bedroom, softly closing the door behind him. I throw my head back on the mattress and let out a frustrated groan. He's trying to kill me. I'm sure of it.

***

Two hours later, we're pushing two carts around the grocery store. I suggested we split up and get what we each needed, but Lucas said we should stick together. I'm not used to being with a man who's so attentive, so of course, I agreed.

"What do you eat for breakfast?" he asks as we turn down the cereal aisle.

"Usually a bagel or yogurt with some granola and fruit. I eat Instant Oatmeal a lot when it's colder outside. All easy-for-one meals. You?"

"Eggs and toast mostly. Gotta get my protein in." He rubs his flat stomach with one hand while pushing his cart with the other.

"Well, if eggs do that—" I nod toward his abs. "—I might need to change my routine."

He chuckles, leans in, and kisses the corner of my mouth, just as a male voice calls out my name.

"Addyson."

Looking over at Lucas, I roll my eyes.

"Addyson," the voice says again, this time closer. I know who it is without turning around, which is why I've yet to turn around.

Pulling my cart in front of Lucas's so we're not blocking the aisle, and so my ex can get through, I finally turn to face him.

Blake.

The guy I dated for months, unaware that he was married.

"How have you been?" he asks. I have to give it to him, he looks genuinely excited to see me.

"Blake," I say flatly. Lucas must recognize the name. He slides in close and places his hand on the small of my back—a silent vow that he stands behind me.

"Moved on already I see." Blake's eyes move to where Lucas has his arm around me.

"It's been five months since we broke up and you're one to talk. Where's your wife, Blake?"

"Getting milk."

He has no limits. I ignore him and look up at Lucas. "We better go. We have lots to do today." I step out of his hold and start toward my cart that's parked in front of his.

"That's it?" Blake calls out. "That's all you've got for me?"

Stopping, I look over my shoulder. "Go to hell, Blake." He blanches as if I've smacked him. I see the hint of a smile on Lucas's face as I turn back around. With my hands gripping my cart, I push forward. I want to turn to see if Blake is gone and if Lucas is following me, but I don't. Instead, I keep my head held high and push on down the aisle.

"Addy." I hear Luke call once I reach the end of the aisle. He slides up beside me with his cart too. I don't know what I was expecting, but it wasn't him leaning in and kissing me softly. "In case I haven't told you, you're amazing." He kisses me again, this time on the corner of my mouth before pulling away. "Next aisle?" he asks. I'm at a loss for words. He's unlike any man I've ever met.

I nod and follow him into the next aisle. That's how the rest of the shopping trip goes. We don't run into Blake or his wife, and I'm happy about that. I'm also thrilled Luke didn't step in all macho and go off on Blake. It's not what I expected of him. He saw that I had it handled and he let me. I knew he was there standing strong beside me if I needed him. His silent support speaks volumes. After the groceries are loaded in the back of his truck and we're on our way to his place, I ask him about it.

"You had it under control. I was there, and no way would I let anything happen to you. He didn't get out of control, and you had it handled." He pauses. "I wanted to punch him," he confesses after a few minutes of silence. "I wanted to wail on him for how he treated you. I thought about it, but then I realized something."

"What's that?" I'm hanging on every word.

"If it were not for Blake being the asshole that he is, I may not have been standing there in that grocery store with you. I may not have been able to hold you in my arms last night. Hell, I may never have met you. So even though I want to hurt him for what he did to you, I want to hurt him for making you lose your trust in yourself and in men, I didn't. His fuck-up gave me you, and for that I'm grateful."

"I don't know what to say to that," I admit. That warmth in my chest is back. It always seems to appear when Lucas is around. Sometimes even when he's not. It's a welcome feeling compared to pain.

He reaches over and lays his hand over mine. "There's nothing to say, Addyson. That's how I feel. I know trust isn't easy for you, so I'm going to show you. All I need you to do is come along for the ride."

"I'm glad you were there that night, eavesdropping on our conversation. Justin has made my best friend happier than I've ever seen. And you, well you're healing my heart." My voice is shaky with my confession. I'm scared to open up, but at the same time, Lucas makes me want to.

"Good." He brings my hand to his lips and kisses my knuckles. "Maybe once it's healed, you'll consider giving it to me." His tone is soft, but the look in his eyes tells me he means every word. He's not laughing or joking. He's being genuine. He's being Lucas.

I think I already have. "Stranger things have happened," I tease, trying to lighten the mood. I'm not ready to confess my feelings. He chuckles at my comment. Luckily, we pull into his place and busy ourselves unloading his groceries. He packs up his laptop and what he needs to work at mine, and we're off again.

The rest of the day is spent lounging around my condo. I get caught up on laundry, and while Lucas works, I make up a chicken noodle casserole. It's a perfect domestic day, and I hate to see it end.

"What time do you have to be at work tomorrow?" I ask.

"Eight, although I'm usually early. You?"

"Same."

"I guess I should get going." We're sitting side by side on my couch, our heads turned, resting against the back of the couch to look at each other.

"Thank you for this weekend, Luke. I had a great time at the rodeo, and last night...." I take a deep breath. Time to give a little. "It was perfect. So much so, I'm not looking forward to sleeping without you."

"Come home with me. Or, if you'd rather be here, I can go grab what I need for work, and come back."

"Are we there yet?" I ask him. This has been fast, but we've been dating for a while now and things are going well.

"I think we're two grown adults who can make decisions based on what's best for them."

"What's best for you?"

"You." His answer is immediate and holds zero hesitation.

"I'm not ready—" His finger landing on my lips stops me.

"I know that. I'm not here to fuck you, Addyson." My eyes widen at his candor, and he grins. "I want to, don't get the two confused. I'm here for you. For us to continue to get to know each other to see where this goes."

"It makes no sense for you to drive home and drive back."

His face falls. He nods and sits up. "Thanks for today." He leans in and kisses me. Just a quick peck on the lips before he stands.

"I like spending time with you," I admit.

"That's good, Addy, because I don't plan on going anywhere."

Not giving myself time to think and worry, I go with my gut. "I'll be right behind you. I just need to pack a few things."

"Wait. What?" he asks, even though I know he heard me, at least if his smile is any indication.

"Unless you've changed your mind."

"No." Firm. Decisive. "I'll wait. Then I'll follow you to my place."

"I'm a big girl, Lucas."

"I know. Humor me, yeah?"

"Give me a few minutes." I jump off the couch and race down the hall to my room. I grab an outfit for tomorrow, some shoes, underwear, bra, and fold them neatly into a small carry-on bag. In another small bag, because I don't want it getting on my clothes, I pack up my shower supplies and makeup. I toss my hair dryer in my larger bag. I'm sure Luke doesn't have one.

"That was fast," he says when I join him in the living room. "Let me carry that." He takes the bags from my hands. Together we leave my place and head toward his. I don't let myself worry. I'm taking the risk slowly. One day at a time.

chapter
eighteen

LUCAS

When I pull into my driveway behind her, I open both garage doors. She must understand my meaning because she pulls her car into the extra bay. I have three attached bays, and I must admit I like the thought of the "extra" bay being hers. Once we're both inside, I close the doors and grab her bags.

"Hungry?" I ask.

"Yeah, I could eat. What are you going to make me?"

"How does a couple of burgers on the grill sound?"

"Delicious actually."

"Good. I'll take these to the bedroom and be right back." I drop a kiss on her cheek, because I can and because I can't not when she's here in my space with me. Rushing down the hall, I place her bags on the bed and grin. I like having her here, having her stuff here.

"What are you doing?" I ask when I see her standing in front of the pantry with the door open.

"Looking for sides. How about mac and cheese?" She holds up a box.

"Perfect." I move in behind her, making sure that I run my hand along her back as I slowly pass. I pull the hamburger meat out of the refrigerator and begin preparing the patties while Addyson starts the mac and cheese.

"So how's work? Last I heard the Covingtons were still causing a ruckus."

I groan. "Unfortunately, yes. They have more money than they know what to do with, and regardless of how many fees we tack on for last-minute changes, she keeps making them. They've already lost one contractor because of it. He kept pushing off jobs thinking he was going to start their build, but the delay with the plans delayed the start date. That means no work for him. So they're now using one of our firm's employed contractors to build, which is a nightmare. I can see changes coming midbuild."

"Yikes. I get wanting it to be perfect, but really, most people have a pretty good idea of what the perfect home looks like."

"Exactly. Speaking of, what's yours?" I ask her.

"Honestly, this place. I love this house and the land. I loved it before I knew who you were. I'd change a few things, but that's paint color and what not. Liven it up a little, but I love it."

"What?" My mouth drops open as if I'm shocked. "My house has life." Her laughter fills the kitchen, and in this moment, my home has never felt more alive.

"It's all… white. Well, except for the bedroom. Did you do that all on your own?"

"I did. My sister, Anna, complained saying it was too… bland and I needed to liven it up a bit. So I painted my bedroom, got some matching bedding, and voila."

"Luke, you put your voila on a room only you see."

"Not true." I step to the sink to wash my hands, then turn to face her. "You see it."

"I don't count."

"You count in every way that matters," I say with conviction.

"Fine, you put your voila on a room only you and I see. I mean, look around you. You have nothing here that makes this place your own. A huge-ass sectional, a matching huge-ass TV, and that's it. You don't even have any family photos."

"I have them… somewhere. Now, you sound like Mom and Anna."

"Maybe you should listen to the women in your life."

"Well, maybe I was waiting on the right woman to come along and help me make this place a home."

"You could be waiting forever. You deserve a home to come home to," she counters.

"I have a house, one I love and designed. I tried to think of everything. Plenty of bedrooms for future kids, and guests. Finished basement for the same thing. Big backyard. The huge-ass bathroom with the crazy big tub, this ginormous kitchen. I tried like hell to make it a place my future wife would want to stay forever."

"You've done that," she says gently. "I'm not denying that. I don't know a single person, male or female, who wouldn't be happy spending forever here. What I'm saying is you need to make it yours too."

"I get what you're saying. What I'm saying is that I want my wife and I to make this place a home together." I watch as a slow smile graces her lips.

"You're one of a kind, Lucas Prescott," she says with admiration. I want to puff out my chest and beat against it with my fists. I made my woman proud. It's caveman, but how I feel all the same.

"Yeah?" I step forward and wrap my arms around her. "What would you say if I told you I hope that woman is you?"

"I'd say you're putting the cart before the horse, bud." She chuckles, tapping my chest lightly.

"Oh, so you're ready to get married? I can do that." I step back, and bend to one knee.

"Luke! Get up." She's now rolling with laughter. "You're crazy."

"Maybe." I grin up at her. I might be crazy because if I thought she'd say yes, I'd ask her. That alone is crazy. I haven't known her long, but I know. And my mamma always said, when you know, you know. Rising to my feet, I place my shoulder at her belly, wrap my hands around her waist and lift her into the air. Stepping out of the way of the refrigerator, I spin her in a circle. This moment alone is worth the ginormous kitchen.

"L-L-Luke," she stutters through her laughter. "Put me down." She smacks my ass.

"Addy, that's only going to make me want to put you down on my bed where I can ravish you."

"Y-you're a beast." She coughs with laughter.

I spin her again, memorizing the sound of her laughter filling my house, making it feel more like a home. Carefully, I place her on the island.

"The stove." She points to where the water for the macaroni noodles is starting to boil over.

Quickly, I step away, turn off the burner, and slide the pot to a back burner. I'm back standing before her, hands resting on her thighs in no time. Her brown eyes capture mine, and I swear I can see myself in her eyes. The love that's beginning to grow between us. I'll wait forever for her to make this place a home with me. There is no timeline except for the one we create on our own.

No words are exchanged between us. None are needed. Sliding my hand behind her neck, I pull her into me. I hover, my lips just a breath away from hers, waiting for her to stop me. She doesn't. She leans in and closes the distance between us, molding her lips with mine. My thumb traces the line of her cheekbone. When she wraps her legs around my waist to hold me close, a rumble from deep in my chest falls from my lips. Pulling her a little closer, I nip at her bottom lip, before soothing it with my tongue.

Time drifts away as my mouth controls hers, her moans urging me forward. I want to get lost in her. Her cell phone rings, effectively lifting the Addyson fog I'm in. Slowly, I end the kiss and pull away. Reaching for her cell phone, I hand it to her, then wrap my arms around her, burying my face in her neck. I'm not ready to end the connection. I caught a glimpse of her swollen red lips, and I want more. More of her kisses. More of her laughter. More of her hugs. I just want fucking more of her. More of Addyson.

"H-hello," she answers.

"Hey, Harp." She listens for a minute. "Actually, I haven't really thought about it." More listening. I can hear mumbling but can't make out what they're saying. "Oh, yeah, I'm at Luke's." I can tell she's smiling, which has me pulling away because I want to see it too. I want to see what a make-out session in my kitchen does to her.

"Harper says hi," she relays to me.

"Hey, Harper," I say, loud enough she can hear me.

"We're just throwing some burgers on the grill," she tells her. "Sure, let me know what night works best for you. We can always go this weekend too." She listens then says goodbye and drops her phone to the counter. "Sorry about that."

"No need to be sorry. It's probably a good thing. I promised to feed you, and well, anymore of that and we would have missed dinner."

"Good thing." Her voice is soft. Breathless. "Anyway, Harper wants to go shopping for the concert."

"Sounds like a girls' day in the making."

"You okay with that?" she questions.

"Are you asking my opinion or my permission?"

"Depends. Do I need your permission?"

"Never," I say sternly. "Addy, you're my girlfriend, not my servant. You had a life before me, and I accept that. All I ask is that you carve a little piece of that life out and let me have it. Let me be a part of it."

"I'm your girlfriend?" she whispers.

"Woman, is that the only thing you got out of that speech? It was a good one," I say, tickling her sides, causing her to squirm. I have mercy on her, move my hands to her hips, and wait for her to calm down and catch her breath. "And yes, you're my girlfriend. I don't want anyone else. I'm not looking, not interested. I only want you." I kiss the tip of her nose.

"Aren't you supposed to ask me that sort of thing?" Her brow quirks in amusement.

"You've already had me on my knees once tonight," I tease, and her cheeks pinken. "How about this?" I cup her face in my hands, my eyes boring into hers. "Addyson Stafford, will you be my girlfriend?"

She giggles. "I think we're past that."

"Hey." I lightly pinch her side, letting my hands fall to the counter, closing her in. "You gonna be my girl or not?"

"I thought I already was."

"Always making me work for it," I mumble, leaning in for a kiss. "Come on, you. We have to get dinner made or we're not going to eat." I lift her from the island and set her on her feet. She goes back to her pot of I'm sure now stuck-together macaroni noodles, and I head out to the back deck to the grill.

A few hours later, with our appetites satisfied—well, for food—and a clean kitchen that my girl insisted on cleaning, we're locking up the house and heading to bed. I follow her into my room and watch as she riffles through the smaller bag.

"Do you care if I set this in the bathroom? It has all of my stuff

I'll need for tomorrow." She pulls out a travel toothbrush container.

"No. In fact, you can leave it here, or buy some to leave here so you're not packing it back and forth all the time."

"You sound like I'm going to be sleeping in your bed more often than not."

"Do I get to cast my vote? If so, then I vote more often."

She smiles. "Thanks, Luke."

"For what?"

"Being you." She grabs the smaller bag and disappears into the bathroom.

Tonight has been very domestic, and I can't say that I hate it. In fact, it's as if this small taste of what our life could be has given me a craving for more.

chapter
nineteen

Addyson

Tonight has been, in a word, perfect. Luke has welcomed me into his home, into his life without reservation. I can't help but think back to my time with Blake. He would tell me his place was small, and his roommate was a dick. Little did I know that roommate was his wife, and his house... turns out wasn't small at all. They live in a two-story in a quiet neighborhood. I was so naive to believe his lies.

I'm grateful Luke didn't give up on me. He was relentless with his pursuit, and here we are. I feel comfortable here, safe with him. He's proven to me, repeatedly, that I come first. Bringing me here after our date, letting me into his life, it's not something I've ever really had. I've never had a man fully committed to me as he seems to be.

Drying off my toothbrush, I place it neatly on the counter. I'll need it again in the morning, so there's no use in putting it away.

I spy the toothbrush holder and think about what he said about leaving things here. On impulse, I drop mine in the holder next to his. I feel giddy at the thought of finally finding a man who's honest and true. Flipping off the bathroom light, I step into the bedroom to find Luke sitting on the edge of the bed.

"All good?" he asks.

"Yes. I'm just going to get changed."

"I think I'll take a quick shower." He stands, kisses my forehead, and passes me for the bathroom. The door clicks softly behind him.

Ruffling through my bag, I pull out the T-shirt and shorts I brought to sleep in. Sliding out of my shorts, I can't help but think about the fact I'm getting naked while he's naked in the next room. Wet and naked. Kicking my shorts to the side, I strip out of my tank and bra. I'm standing in his room in just my panties. Glancing at the sleep clothes waiting for me on the bed, I make an impulsive decision. Sliding my panties down my legs, I kick them to the side and turn to face the bathroom door.

One foot after the other, I slowly make my way to the door. Cautiously, I reach for the handle and give it a turn. It opens. I can hear the shower running as I step into the room. Pushing the door closed, leaving just a small crack, I softly pad my way to the shower. Luke has his back to me, so I take a minute to take him in. It's obvious he works out and takes care of his body. He has muscle definition that I've only ever seen in fitness magazines.

His shower is huge, so huge that it doesn't have doors or a curtain. It's a tile hallway of sorts. Black, white, and gray tiles line the walls. There is a bench on one end and more jets that I care to take the time to count. Stepping over the ledge, I walk toward him. His head is tilted forward, letting the water rain down on him. Tentatively, I reach out and trace my hand down his back. Slowly, his head lifts, and he turns to look at me over his shoulder.

His eyes are liquid pools of desire. "Addyson," he croaks.

Another step forward.

I wrap my arms around his waist and rest my cheek on his back. His large hands cover mine. Neither one of us moves, soaking in the moment for what it is, what it means. I'm letting him in. I've dropped all my protective barriers when it comes to Luke, and I'm choosing to trust him. To trust in this uncontrollable want that I have for him. I've felt the connection since the night we met, and no matter how much I fight it, it remains.

I can't turn back now.

My heart's invested.

With a gentle grip on my hands, he pulls them free of his body and turns to face me. "Jesus," he murmurs.

With rapt attention, I watch as he takes me in. I fight the urge to fidget under his hot gaze, but when he looks up, his brown eyes colliding with mine, I'm frozen in time. Frozen in this moment. He's looking at me with… adoration, and something more. Something, I don't want to think about. Not right now. Not tonight.

"Luke." My voice is raspy. His eyes snap to mine. "Show me."

"Show you what, baby?" He tilts his head to the side, studying me.

"That you're the difference."

I watch him closely as he swallows hard and nods. Then with shaking hands, he reaches out and tenderly palms both of my breasts in his large hands. He runs the pad of his thumb over my nipples, and my knees go weak. Arms stretched out, I brace myself on the wall of the shower. He dips his head and slides his tongue over one nipple while rolling the other between his thumb and his forefinger. Pleasure races through me, and it's unlike anything I've ever felt before.

He takes his time, ravishing one breast and then the other. Back and forth, giving them both equal attention while driving me insane with need. For him. "Luke." My voice is pleading.

His head lifts and his eyes find mine. His chest is rapidly rising and falling, his eyes on fire. A small gasp flies from my mouth when he places his hands on my hips, lifts me from the tiled floor, and turns us. He lifts me so I'm standing on the bench. The jets keep us warm with the hot spray of water, not that we need it. I'm on fire for him, and the look in his eyes tells me it's the same for Luke.

He lightly caresses my hips and the back of my thighs. When he leans in and kisses me, just below my belly button, a whimper escapes me. "Your skin is so soft," he murmurs, his hands taking the same path they just traveled. Up the back of my thighs, over my hips, and to my waist, then back again.

Hands grip the back of my thighs, and he looks up at me. "Spread your legs." I do as he asks, although my knees are trembling in anticipation. "Brace your hands on my shoulders." Again, I oblige. He steps in close, so close that his head rests against my chest, one hand still gripping my thigh, tethering me to him, while the other begins to roam. When his finger traces through my folds, I'm certain my legs would have buckled if not for the firm grip he has on me.

"Luke," I call out for him. His head snaps up. Keeping one hand on his shoulder for balance, I run the other through his hair. "I'm yours. Don't hold back."

"Addy." He pauses. "I want more than just this." His fingers once again make their way through my folds. "I want all of you. I want your mind, your spirit, your laughter. I want your body, but most of all, baby, I want your heart." He stares deeply into my eyes, willing me to trust him.

"You have all of me," I assure him. It's not a declaration of love, but it's the best I can do. I'm opening myself to him and the possibility of a future together. And even though I'm scared out of my mind, there is something deep inside my soul that tells me Lucas Prescott is a man I can count on.

"That's good, baby," he rasps as he slides a digit inside of me. "Because you own me." He's done talking as his lips travel across my chest, capturing a nipple, all while his magical fingers bring me to the edge. His mouth is hot, his teeth lethal, his tongue soothing as he makes love to my breasts. His hand, the one between my thighs, feels as though it's larger than life. His thumb strums my clit, while he slides another digit inside of me. My body is on sensation overload.

"Luke." I throw my head back with a moan. With each pump of his fingers, I want to tell him I need him inside of me. Right. Now. However, my words fail me. Instead, a cry tears from my throat as my orgasm rushes through me. My nails dig into his shoulder as I hold on for the ride.

When I finally find the power to open my eyes, it's to find his trained on me. "You're beautiful," he murmurs, placing a kiss on my chest, right over my heart.

"I need more of you, Luke."

"Tell me what you want, what you need."

He needs to hear me say it. I've been keeping him at arm's length for so long, he needs confirmation that this is what I want. That *he* is who I want.

"I need you inside me." I watch as he swallows hard before he slowly releases his arms from around my waist and backs away.

"Lucas?" I ask, and even I can hear the panic in my voice.

"Condom," he rasps.

"No," I say before thinking.

He freezes. "Addyson?"

I told him I was all-in. "I'm clean," I say, holding my hand out for him. He takes it, and steps in close, wrapping his arms around me once again. I sigh at the contact as this is where he belongs. Where we belong. Together. "It's been months. My last was Blake and I was checked. You know… the cheating thing." I shrug. "I've never…" I shake my head. Why is this awkward?

"Not without protection," I finish.

"It's never been worth the risk," he says. "Never wanted to be tied to someone like I do you. I'm clean too."

"I'm on the pill," I add since there's more than just diseases to talk about.

"Good to know, but I don't care about that."

"What?" I lean back, his words surprising me.

"The thought of a tiny human that's a part of both of us isn't an unpleasant idea." He shrugs, and if I'm not mistaken, a slight blush coats his cheeks. It's hard to tell from the hot shower raining down on us and the intense desire that radiates between us, but I'm pretty certain it's a blush.

"We're covered all the same," I assure him. I'm not quite sure what else there is to say. My walls have shattered, crumbled to tiny little shards of glass around my heart. This strong, confident, loving man is telling me he wouldn't have a problem being bound to me for life. That's intense, and more than what I bargained for when I walked into this shower.

"Are you sure you want this?" He gives me an out. Something only Luke has ever offered me.

"I want this."

He nods. "Put your arms around my neck." I do as he asks. "Legs around my waist," he says when he lifts me from the bench seat. I wrap around him like a monkey. "I can't go slow right now. I want to," he says huskily. "I want to make love to you, but I can't this time. I'm ready to lose my mind, and I already know without a doubt that when my cock slides inside of you, it's not going to take long for me to fall over the edge."

"We can make it up next time." A rush of heat courses through me at his confession. I just need to feel him inside of me.

His eyes heat. "Next time," he agrees as he pushes his hard length inside of me for the first time. "Fuck," he moans, resting his forehead on my shoulder. I've never felt this... full before. I hold on tight as my body adjusts to his size. Needing more, I rock my hips, letting him know I'm ready. He spins us around, and I squeal as he pushes my back against the shower wall. "Hold on to me. Don't let go," he warns with a barely controlled edge to his voice. He gives me everything he has. Over and over, thrust after thrust, he fills me, bringing me to the edge of release. All I can do is hold on and enjoy the ride.

"I'm... fuck—" Thrust. "Close," he grits out. His voice is gruff as his hands tighten on my thighs.

I don't reply. I can't. My orgasm steals my ability to speak. That is until I cry out his name as the most intense release of my life washes over me. I can do nothing but hold on as I ride wave after wave of pleasure that crashes into me. My entire body is rocked to the core, as ecstasy races through my veins. Everything is heightened, the feel of his hard cock plunging in and out of me, the grip of his hands on my thighs, and the way his shoulders flex beneath the palms of my hands. When he calls out my name, it's a deep, gritty sound as he gives me one final thrust before he pulses inside me. My body quakes again, spasming around him, taking everything he's giving me.

Chest to chest, heart to heart, we're both laboring to catch our breaths. His strong arms wrap around me, and he moves us to the bench. He settles there, never losing his hold on me. He's still inside of me, my legs are still around his waist, and my body still hums from the aftershock of what we just experienced.

"My knees are weak," he pants, breaking the silence. "I've never felt anything like that."

"Mmm," I reply. I want to say more, but I can't seem to form the words. Not that I would know how to describe what just happened between us. It was nothing short of magical.

His grip loosens, and his hands are cupping my cheeks. I open my eyes to find his intense stare. "Never, Addyson. Do you hear me?" His brown eyes watch me intently, willing me to hear and believe what he's saying.

"For me too," is my whispered confession. I'm not even sure

if he hears me as my voice is so soft and the water from his massive shower still rains down on us.

I'm not sure how long we sit here, embracing each other like our lives depend on it, but eventually, Luke stands, sliding from my body and helping me steady my feet on the shower floor. "Let's get you cleaned up." He steps away from me and grins. "If I stay that close to you, we're never getting out of this shower."

"It is roomy." I smile.

"Addyson," he groans. "Shower and get your fine ass in bed. We both have to be up early tomorrow."

"Who would have thought you'd be the voice of reason in this relationship," I quip, reaching for some of his bodywash. Mine is in my bag on the counter, but I like the thought of smelling like him.

He just smiles at me, kissing my forehead. His eyes are bright as he reaches for the bodywash that's in my hands. Quickly, we finish our shower and turn off the water. Lucas steps out first, wrapping a towel around his waist, and then one around me. He's dried off in no time, dropping a kiss to my temple and disappearing into the bedroom. I take my time toweling off, giving myself time to reflect on what just happened between us. I brush out my hair and tie it in a knot on top of my head. I'm sure it will be a hot mess in the morning, but I can't seem to find it in me to care. I don't have clothes in here, and really after what we just shared it feels silly to even want them. Taking a deep breath, I slowly exhale, accepting that I'm trusting him with my heart. It's too late to turn back now. Turning off the light, I step out of the bathroom in search of Luke.

I find him standing on his side of the bed, still naked and sliding under the covers. "My bag?" I ask him.

"I put it in the closet. I hung up your clothes. Come to bed." He pulls the cover back and holds it open for me. Not needing to be told twice, I slide in beside him. He meets me in the middle of his huge-ass bed and wraps his naked body around mine. "Night, Addy."

"Night, Luke," I whisper just before sleep claims me.

chapter
twenty

LUCAS

It's Saturday, and I've spent my morning doing yard work. Addyson and Harper went shopping, and there was mention of stopping to get their toes done. According to Harper, going to the Dan + Shay concert next weekend requires a new outfit. I have a feeling, it's less about the outfit and more about spending the day together. Justin and I have been monopolizing their time, and they don't see as much of each other as they used to.

I told them to just come over here when they're done. Justin is going to be here around six, and we'll throw some steaks and chicken breasts on the grill, swim, and just catch up. However, before that, I have some errands to run. My first stop is my parents. It's been a couple of weeks since I've stopped by, which isn't like me at all. When Ollie, my nephew, called me a couple of hours ago and asked if I was mad at him, I knew I'd fucked up. I promised him as soon as the yard work was done, I'd come to toss the football with him. He's with my parents today since Anna had to work.

As soon as I pull into my parents' driveway, he's flying out the door, down the front steps, and is waiting at the door of my truck, football in hand. "Hey, buddy." I reach down and pick him up. He's small for six, but I was too at his age.

"Ready?" he asks, his eyes full of excitement.

"Yeah, bud." I set him back on his feet, and he takes off for the front yard. We spend the next thirty minutes tossing the ball. Well, there's more chasing than anything on my end, but he's only six. He'll get there.

"Ollie," my sister Anna calls out for him. "Time for lunch."

He doesn't talk back or whine. He simply nods and, with his football under his arm, heads inside to get cleaned up. He's such a good kid, and I feel bad I've gone this long without seeing him. His dad left when he was just a few weeks old. He sees him every other weekend and during the week when Anna needs the help. Although it's as if she has to pull teeth to get him to actually do more than his every-other-weekend visit. The worst part? He has a new baby, a new wife, and he seems to be very attentive to them. At least for now. Only time will tell if he'll walk out on her like he did my sister. I get it. Hearts change, you fall out of love, but your kid? That's life. You don't get the option to walk away. You're man enough to create a life, you're man enough to care for that child. There are no exceptions to that rule.

"You hungry?" Mom asks when I enter the kitchen.

"Always." I laugh, messing up Ollie's hair as I pass his seat at the table.

"Help yourself." Mom points to the counter where all the fixings for lunchmeat sandwiches are laid out. Not needing to be told twice, I make a couple of sandwiches and take a seat at the table.

"Where's Dad?"

"He and Tom are golfing today. He'll be sorry that he missed you."

"It's a good day for it."

"We haven't seen you much lately," she says.

She's baiting me. "Just been busy," I say casually, knowing it will drive her crazy.

"When do I get to meet her?" she blurts before taking a bite of her sandwich.

"Soon." I shake my head at her. "I don't need you scaring her off."

"Me?" She acts as though I've offended her. We both know better.

"Yes, you," Anna chimes in. "We know how protective you can get, mama bear." She laughs and looks over at her son. "I get it."

Mom looks wide-eyed and innocent. "I promise to be good."

"Soon," I repeat, trying to appease her.

She studies me a moment. "You're smitten," she gushes.

"Mom, give him a break." My sister defends me.

"No." I wave Anna off. "She's right, but it's more than just smitten, Mom. I really like her. She's been hurt in the past, and I'm taking things slowly. I want you to meet her. We just need a little more time." Truth is, things have been so great with us, I'm afraid to jinx us. Not that my family would ever do that, but the worry is there. Smitten doesn't quite describe how I feel for her. No, the only word suitable is love.

I'm in love with her.

"Fine," Mom concedes, completely unaware of what I've just admitted to myself. Not that she would know. I'm completely calm. There is zero panic rolling around in my head; instead, it's thoughts of mine and Addy's future. One I feel stronger about every day.

Once we've finished eating, Anna takes Ollie upstairs to get cleaned up, and I help Mom in the kitchen. "Tell Dad I'm sorry I missed him."

"Will do. I'm sure he'll be sorry he missed you."

"I'll stop by one night next week." Even as I say the words, I'm wondering if I can bring Addy with me or if it's still too soon like I claimed it to be a few minutes ago. The alternative is not seeing her. Maybe I can leave work early and still make it back to my place at the usual time.

After a quick hug and a yell of goodbye up the steps, I'm back in my truck and headed to my next stop. I'm barely home ten minutes when I hear a car pull into the drive. Glancing out the kitchen window, I see it's Addyson. I move to the garage and open the door for her. She pulls her car into her spot and climbs out. I'm there waiting for her. "Hey." I snake my arm around her waist and kiss her hello. "Where's Harper?"

"I dropped her off at Justin's. They'll be here in a couple of hours."

"You need help carrying anything in?"

"Luke, at this rate, I'm going to have more of my belongings here than at my place."

"I like that plan," I admit.

She shakes her head in disbelief, but there is a small smile playing on her lips. "I just have two bags, so I can manage." She opens the back door and pulls out two bags.

Hitting the button on the garage door, I follow her into the house. "Did you have a good day?" I guide her to the couch once she sets the bags down on the kitchen island.

"Yes. It's been a while since Harper and I have spent the day together."

I take a seat on the couch, and pull her down on my lap, snuggling her close. "I missed you."

"I was gone a few hours."

"It's four in the afternoon. You left at nine."

"That's less than a workday," she counters.

"Too damn long," I grumble, pulling her closer.

"Do we have everything we need for tonight? Do we need to run to the store?"

I don't comment on how she says we instead of me, joining us together, as if this is our home and we're having guests over. A man can dream. "No, we're good. I have chicken and steaks. Justin was going to grab some beer, and whatever else he thinks we need."

"What else are we having?" She turns to face me.

I lean in for a kiss, which she accepts willingly. When I pull away, I say, "Salad, baked potatoes, and whatever else he comes up with."

"Do we have dressing? I know we were out." A sexy blush covers her cheeks. It's finally dawned on her how it sounds.

"Yeah, baby, we're good. I picked some up when I was out today."

She looks away. I'm sure embarrassed, even though she has no reason to be. I want our lives to be one. "Luke," she says softly. That's when I know she sees what I picked up today.

"You might not live here, not officially, not yet, and I know you're not ready for that," I rush to say. "But I thought it was time we started turning this house into a home. Besides, you make it feel that way. I love having you here."

She stands and walks toward the framed picture on the mantel. The one and only picture in my house. I watch as she picks it up and studies it. Not able to stand being away from her, I go to her, wrapping my arms around her waist and resting my chin on top of her head. "We look good together."

"Yeah," she agrees, taking in the image of us from the benefit a few weeks ago.

"We make a good team."

I can hear her sniff. "I'm ridiculous," she says with laughter in her voice. "This picture shouldn't have me in tears."

"Are you happy, Addyson?"

She turns in my arms. "Incredibly."

"Good. Then when you're ready, you can add your own pictures next to mine." I kiss her forehead. "Now, we have about two hours before they get here. I say we take a nap."

"Right." She laughs. "Nap."

"No, really, I'm beat. I mowed the yard, ran the weed eater, and then tossed the football with Ollie for about thirty minutes. I'm exhausted."

"Poor baby," she coos.

"They want to meet you," I say, testing the waters. "My family wants to meet you."

"I'd like to meet them too."

"Yeah?" I ask in disbelief.

"We're doing this, so I'm going to have to meet them at some point. Just tell me when and I'll be there."

"I'll set it up. You should plan on doing the same," I tell her. "Now, about that nap." Clasping my hand around hers, I guide her down the hall to the bedroom. We don't bother stripping out of our clothes as we climb on the bed. Before long, we drift off to sleep.

***

The sound of the doorbell wakes me. Peeling open my eyes, I peer over Addy and look at the alarm clock on her nightstand. Five after six. Shit. We slept late. Placing a kiss on her cheek, I pull myself away from her to go answer the door.

"Hey," I say, greeting Justin and Harper. "Come on in. I'll be just a second." I close the door behind them and head back to my room. Addyson is sitting on the edge of the bed, hand over her mouth covering a yawn.

"I didn't think we'd sleep that long. Actually, I didn't think we would sleep." She grins.

"Yeah, well, don't go looking all cute or our friends might

have to entertain themselves," I say, stepping to stand in front of her.

"No, sir." She lays her hands on my chest and pushes me back. "No, that is not going to happen when we have, I mean, when you have guests in the other room." We have guests, in our home. She may not call my house home, not yet, but we're getting there.

"I can be quiet." I step forward again.

She hops off the bed, and steps around me, going to the door. "You might be able to, but I can't." She winks before rushing out the door. I hear her greet our friends and then laughter carries down the hall. Hers I can pick out among the others. It's a sound that seems to have brought this house, brought *me* to life. I never want to lose it. Flipping off the light, I head down the hall. I find them in the living room. Harper and Justin are sitting on the couch while Addyson is in the chair. I walk to where she's sitting and lean against the arm of the chair.

"Hope we didn't interrupt." Harper wags her eyebrows.

"Not this time," I say, causing Addyson to smack my leg playfully.

"We were sleeping," she tells her best friend.

"Is that what we're calling it these days?" Justin jokes.

"Trust me, if it were anything else, your ass would still be standing on my front porch."

"I have a key, remember."

"Yeah, well. Use it with caution, my friend," I warn him, and the four of us cut up with laughter.

The remainder of the night is low-key. Dinner, laughing, talking, and enjoying great company. Justin and I have done this—just hanging out—a thousand times, but I must admit it's so much better when the love of your life is by your side.

Now I just need to find the right time to tell her.

chapter
twenty-one

Addyson

It's the day of the concert, and Harper and I decided we needed to get ready together. Like old times. The guys didn't give us too much of a fuss. In fact, Justin offered his place and fled to Luke's.

"Remind me again why we couldn't have done this at either my place or yours?" I ask Harper.

"He likes me here." She looks at me in the mirror.

We're currently in the master bath doing our hair and makeup. "What about you? Do you like it here?"

Her eyes meet mine again. "I never want to leave. Not because of the house, but because of Just. I love him, Addy," she confesses, turning to face me.

I wrap my arms around her in a hug. "I'm so happy for you."

"Thanks. It's fast, you know, but I don't really care. I know what I feel."

"There is no timeline," I say, quoting Luke's words to me.

"Yeah, I like that." She nods and turns back to the mirror. "What about you? If I recall, my boyfriend isn't the only one who offered up his house."

"I trust him." Three words I never thought I would be able to say again.

"Wow." She turns to look at me. "Addyson, that's huge."

I nod. "I know, but he's so open, and there's something in his eyes, you know? It's the way he looks at me, and the way he touches me, like I'm something precious to him. I've never been on the receiving end of that."

"Remind me to give that man a hug." She laughs. "He brought back the light in your eyes."

"I love him," I repeat her earlier words. Surprisingly there is no panic, no fear of waiting for the other shoe to drop. Not with Luke.

"Have you told him?" she asks, excited.

"Have you?" I counter.

"Yes."

"No."

"Are you going to?" she questions.

"I don't know," I confess. Telling my best friend and telling Lucas are two completely different situations.

"He loves you, you know that, right?"

"I know."

"Then what's holding you back?"

"I'm not sure. I guess I've been hurt so many times I'm just working up the courage to put myself out there again."

"Too late for that. You've already put yourself out there. Everything but actually ending the suspense for that man and telling him how you feel."

"When did you tell Justin?"

"Every day." She smiles. "About a month ago."

"I'll let you slide on not telling your best friend." I give her a pointed look.

"Good for you." I smile at her in the mirror.

"Good for us. All of us. Who would have thought drinks at Stagger would have ended up with both of us finding love? And I wasn't intentionally not telling you. It's just things have been happening so fast for both of us. It just kind of happened and kept happening."

"Right? Not in a million years, and I forgive you. I'm so happy for you, Harper."

"I wouldn't change it."

"Not for anything," I agree. We finish getting ready while laughing and catching up. We've just slipped on our boots when we hear the front door open and close.

"Harp, babe, you ready?" Justin calls up the steps.

"You ready?" she asks me.

"Yep." I take one final look in the mirror. My hair is full of loose curls pulled into a side ponytail. I decided on a brown sundress with teal accents to match the teal in my cowboy boots. Harper is wearing a blue denim skirt and a pink halter-style top, and her boots are black and pink. We look like the coordinating small-town girls that we are.

Grabbing my phone and small crossbody, I shove the rest of my things in my bag and follow Harper downstairs. "Addy." Luke holds his hand out for me, and I go to him. He raises our joined hands in the air and spins me around. "You're beautiful." His eyes rake over me.

"Stop that," I scold him playfully.

"What?" His brows dip low.

"Looking at me like that. We're leaving for a concert."

"And?"

"And…" I blow out a hot breath. "That look, it does things to me… every time you look at me like that."

"Like what?" he whispers, his lips next to my ear.

"Like you want to devour me," I reply just as softly.

"I don't know how to stop it. I do want to devour you."

Yes, please.

"Ready?" Harper asks over her shoulder. She and Justin are standing at the door waiting on us.

"Yes." Luke takes my bag and puts it in the back seat of his truck, locking the doors. We climb into the back seat of Justin's truck, and hit the road. Harper and I pregame, if that's what you want to call it. She connects her phone to the truck's radio and plays DJ. We go from listening to Shaggy to Charlie Puth to Dan + Shay. Of course, we had to work them in since that's where we're headed. The guys laugh at us and sing along with our little truck-ride concert.

We arrive at the arena two hours before the show starts. The tickets Justin snagged are VIP, which means we get to meet Dan + Shay. I'm pumped about it, but not nearly as excited as Harper. She's texted me all week since our shopping trip. Justin pulls his truck into VIP parking and kills the engine.

"Ready for the preshow festivities?" he asks Harper.

She squeals and lunges over the console to kiss him. "You know you're the best boyfriend ever, right?" she asks him, pulling away.

"Hear that, Luke?" Justin laughs.

"I heard, Romeo. Let's get moving so we can get this over with."

"What? You're not excited?" I tease.

"Excited to see my girl fawn all over other men? Yeah, not so much. However, I am excited to be here with you, so let's get this show on the road." He reaches for the door handle and climbs down out of the truck. He offers me his hand, so I slide across the seat, and instead of letting me take his hand, he grips my hips and lifts me from the truck. His lips connect with mine briefly before he sets me on the ground. Hand in hand, we follow Justin and Harper to the entrance gate. Justin flashes them our tickets, and we're each given VIP lanyards that will give us access to backstage as well as the VIP section for drinks and bathrooms. A pretty sweet deal that I'm sure Harper and I would never have splurged on had it been us.

"Hey, Justin," I call up to him. They stop and turn to look at me. "Please let me pay you something for the tickets."

He grins. "They were free." He shrugs.

"Come on, just tell me how much," I counter.

"Addy," Luke says beside me. "He's telling the truth. Justin's family is prominent in the business world. He didn't have to pay anything."

"Really?" Harper and I ask at the same time.

"Really," he assures us, then turns to Harper. "I know I've told you my family is well off, but I didn't exactly tell you how well off."

"Just because your family has money doesn't mean I can't repay you for the tickets."

"One, I didn't pay a dime and two, I wouldn't let you even if I did. Have you ever heard of Atwood Enterprises?" Her mouth drops open. "Yeah." He smiles sheepishly. "My family, my grandfather to be exact, started the company. Now we're the largest fast food supply chain in the country."

"Wow," she breathes. "I-I had no idea," she says softly as she drops his hand and wraps her arms around her waist.

"Hey." He steps close, but she takes another step back.

I feel like I should turn away to give them privacy, but I don't. Instead, I watch her, gauging her reaction. If I need to get her out of here, I won't hesitate. There will be other concerts.

"Harp," Justin sighs. "What's wrong?"

"Nothing's wrong," she replies. "I just... didn't expect you to drop that tidbit of info on me. Your parents seem too nice, normal even." She laughs. "Are you sure they're okay with us dating? I mean, I'm just this small-town girl."

I watch as a slow smile that turns megawatt crosses his face. "I love you, Harper. That's what matters. For the record, I don't give a fuck what my parents say or think. I'm not in the family business, as you know. However, just because we have money does not mean that we're stuck-up snobs. They love you, trust me, they would let me know if they felt otherwise. They just want me to be happy, and you make me happy. That's all that matters." He takes a step forward, and this time, she doesn't move. That's progress. "That you couldn't care less about the fact that we have money makes you perfect for me."

"Of course, I don't care," she says, offended. "I didn't fall in love with your bank account. I fell in love with you for who you are, for how you respect me, how you treat me." She drops her arms to her sides, and I know they're going to be okay.

I turn my back to them, and Luke does the same. "They're good together," he says, wrapping his arms around me from behind.

"They are."

"So are we."

I turn, needing to see his face. Reaching up, I run my fingers over his week-long beard. "We are," I say, just before standing on my tiptoes and kissing him.

"You plan on making out all night or are we going to see a concert?" Harper calls out a few minutes later.

"Bring on the hotness!" I cheer, causing both Luke and Justin to grumble in defeat.

Harper grabs me by the hand and links her arm through mine. The guys fall in behind us as we lead the way to our backstage experience.

***

"Gah! I can't believe we got hugs from both of them," Harper gushes.

"Right? Justin, thank you so much," I say, wrapping my arms around Luke's waist.

"Sure, no problem. I'm the world's biggest idiot," he grumbles.

"What's that?" I ask.

"I said, I'm the world's biggest idiot."

"Why would you say that?" Harper asks, concern lacing her voice.

"Because I made it possible for those men to put their hands on you."

I can't help it, I burst out laughing. He sounds so sad. "They're married, Justin. Both of them. Not to mention, we're kind of taken," I remind him.

"You're damn right you are," Luke says, his lips next to my ear. "I don't plan on letting you forget it."

"I don't want to," I assure him.

"We better go find our seats," Justin says, smiling down at Harper. She must have eased his fears while I was wrapped up in Luke. Worming our way through the crowd, we make it to our section. We're in the bottom row of the midlevel.

"They offered me floor, but I just assumed you didn't want to deal with being pushed around all night," Justin says, pointing down to the pit.

"These are perfect. A great view of the stage, and…" Harper pulls out her phone and zooms in. "The pictures are going to be awesome," she says excitedly.

The opening act, a band I've never heard of, takes the stage and we settle in our seats. Luke places his arm on the back of my seat, and I snuggle in close with a smile on my face. A smile that he put there. I never thought I would fall again, especially so quickly. But it is Luke, and well, everything with Luke is as natural as it is easy.

chapter
twenty-two

LUCAS

I don't think I've ever had this much fun at a concert. I'm not even drinking. None of us are. Justin and I made sure that he and I would be driving and told the girls to have at it, but they both declined, opting for bottles of water instead. The night's flying by, and it's been a blast. That has everything to do with the amazing woman shaking her ass to the beat.

My girlfriend.

My future.

At least I hope so. With each passing day, she breaks off another little piece of my heart and makes it her own. Not that I care. I'm handing it over on a silver platter. It's hers for the taking. She does a little shimmy and her fine ass brushes against my cock. Snaking an arm around her waist, I pull her against me and sway my hips to the beat. "You have to stop this," I say, nipping her earlobe. She's turning me on with all these sexy little moves. Who am I kidding? If she's breathing, I'm turned on. It's not something I can control; it's just Addyson and her effect on me.

My lips travel down to her neck, which she's so conveniently exposed for me tonight with her hair pulled to one side. Her head falls back to rest against my chest, and her head tilts to the side. I take advantage and trace the long slender column with my tongue. I don't give a fuck that we're in public. Everyone around us is dancing and standing on their feet. Hell, most of them are so damn drunk they're either being loud and obnoxious or practically fucking their date, so they're not worried about what I'm doing. Not that I care. Not when it comes to Addyson and getting my mouth and hands on her.

She turns in my arms, wraps her arms around my neck and begins to sway, just as the song changes. "I love this one." She smiles up at me as Dan + Shay begin to sing their hit "Speechless."

Pulling her close, I whisper the words in her ear. Every damn line of this song is us. It's me for her. It's cliché as hell, but it is what it is. We're standing still in a crowd of thousands, but all I see is her. When the song ends, she lifts her head, and I can see it in her eyes. She feels it. The love that I have for her is impossible to miss. I can't hide it nor do I want to. Resting my forehead against hers, I'm going to tell her. I know she might not say it back, but I can't pass up this moment. My heart needs her to hear it. I open my mouth to speak, but she beats me to it.

"I love you." Her voice is clear. Strong.

The breath expels from my lungs as I crush her to me, lifting her off her feet. She giggles, burying her face in my neck. "Say it again."

Lifting her head, she places her hands on either side of my face. "I love you, Lucas Prescott."

"I love you too, so fucking much. I love you." I kiss her hard. Someone behind us yells for us to get a room, followed by laughter and catcalls. She breaks our kiss and smiles up at me, before turning back around and watching the rest of the show. She dances some more, driving me insane.

On the drive back to Justin's, she sits close tucked into my side. My arm's around her shoulders while the four of us talk about the show. It's mostly Addy and Harper who are chatting, but Justin and I chime in when we can.

"You guys want to come in?" Justin offers.

"No, thanks." I'm quick to decline. I chance a look at Addyson who's standing beside me on the driveway. She doesn't seem to be upset.

"I'm exhausted," she says, stepping forward and hugging Justin, then Harper. The girls exchange whispered words, and when they pull away, both are all smiles.

"Stay put," I say, driving into the garage at my place. I'm quick to climb out of the truck and rush to her door. Pulling it open, I lean in and kiss her.

"We gonna stay out here all night?" she asks against my lips.

"No. Definitely not." Hands on her hips, I lift her from the truck and set her on her feet.

"You know, I can get myself in and out of your truck."

"You're tiny," I counter.

Her hands go to her hips, and she gives me a "you did not just say that" look. "I'm built low for stability," she says, barely able to contain her grin. Her lip is twitching as is mine.

"Stability, huh?" I ask her.

"Yes." She stands a little taller.

"How's this for stability?" Bending down, I put my shoulder in her belly and lift her off the ground.

"Luke!" She laughs. "Put me down."

"Nope. I think I'll keep you. In fact, you might just fit in my pocket," I tease her. She smacks my ass. "That's not going to convince me to put you down, babe."

She grumbles then clears her throat. "Please, put me down." Her voice is sugary sweet.

"Nope."

"Luke," she says.

"Addy?"

"I love you," she says loud and clear, just as I enter my bedroom.

I toss her on the bed, and lean over her, caging her in with my hands on either side of her head. Brown eyes stare up at me. "I." *Kiss.* "Love." *Kiss.* "You." *Kiss.* "Too." *Kiss.* "You know what else?" I ask as I kiss down her neck.

"W-what?"

"I'm going to make love to you," I whisper in her ear.

She sucks in a breath. "I like this plan." She tilts her head to the side.

"Good." Pushing back, I stand to my full height. "Strip."

A wicked grin crosses her face as she lifts herself up onto her elbows. "That's not very make love-ish."

I chuckle. "Is love-ish a word?"

"It is now."

"Strip, Addy." I offer her my hand to help her off the bed. "I need you naked for what I plan to do to you." That's all the motivation she needs to hop off the bed and strip out of her clothes. I do the same, but I'm sure to keep my eyes on her as she peels back each layer. When she steps toward me, I watch her facial expression, trying to gauge what she's thinking. That is until all thoughts leave my brain when she wraps her small hands around my cock.

"Luke?" she asks softly.

I swallow hard. "Addy."

"What if I don't want you to make love to me? What if I want something else?"

"Name it." If it's within my power, it's hers.

"I want you," she says, and my reply is immediate.

"You have me, baby."

"I wasn't finished." She tsks with her tongue. "What I was going to say…" She strokes me lightly from root to tip. It's simple, basic compared to being inside of her, but her hands are soft, and this is Addyson, so of course it turns me on. "That I want you in my mouth," she finishes as she drops to her knees.

Her hot breath touches my shaft. "Addy, you don't have to do this. Let me take care of you." Even I can hear the desperation in my voice. I'm too amped up from our night, from the knowledge that this beautiful woman loves me back. I'll lose control with her mouth on me.

She peers up at me under her lashes. I push her hair back from her face so I can see her clearly. "That's what this is about, Lucas. Me and you taking care of each other." Before I can reply, she has her mouth on me.

Sexy as fuck.

Her hands and mouth drive me out of my mind. Stroke after stroke. Lick after lick. She's giving me the best blow job of my life, and I don't even want to think about where she learned the skill or the fuckers who threw her away after. Pushing that out of my mind, I lock my knees, gather her hair in my hands, and enjoy the ride.

"Addy," I say through gritted teeth. "S-stop." I manage to push the words past my lips.

She doesn't stop. She continues to bob her head, and that sight alone pushes me over the edge. With no more warning, I spill into her hot, wet mouth. Pulse after pulse. Her eyes are closed as she swallows down everything I'm giving her. It's not until my cock falls from her mouth and she wipes the back of her hand across her reddened lips that I realize the iron grip I have on her hair. "I'm sorry." I remove my hand from the silky strands.

"I loved it. It's a heady feeling knowing I can drive a man like you to lose his mind."

"Come here." I hold out my hand. She stands, and I pull her naked body into mine. My voice is gravelly when I say, "I don't know what you mean by a man like me, but I can tell you that you're the only woman who's ever made me lose my mind."

"It's a gift." She chuckles.

Releasing her from my hold, I turn toward the bed and pull back the covers. "After you."

"I wore you out, huh?" She smirks.

"I need a few minutes," I tell her. "But I'm far from worn out. Get your fine ass in this bed."

She shimmies said naked ass and then climbs into bed, burrowing under the covers. I follow her, pulling her into me. Her skin is soft like silk, and my hands roam over every inch they can reach.

"You're so warm." She snuggles in closer. "Your house is like an icebox."

"Babe, it's ninety degrees outside and you're naked."

"It's like forty in here," she counters, resting her head on my chest.

"I'll go turn it up." I reach for the cover, but she stops me.

"No. Stay. You're warming me up," she says huskily, running her foot up my leg.

"I can warm you up." I roll over on top of her. Her legs open for me and I settle between them. Right where I'm meant to be. Resting my weight on my elbows, I smooth her hair out of her face. The glow of the moonlight streaming through the windows is enough for me to make out her features. "We had a big night tonight."

"We did." I can hear the smile in her voice.

"I've known for a while now," I confess. "I was too afraid to tell you. I didn't want to scare you away."

"I've known but was too afraid to tell you. Not because I didn't think you felt it too. I could see it in the way you look at me. My past..." She exhales before continuing. "It's not going to determine my future. I'm trusting you with my heart, Luke."

"It's safe with me, and so are you." She lifts her head, meeting me in a slow, sensual kiss as I slide inside of her. She exhales as if us being joined in the most intimate way brings her peace. Remaining still, I can feel her pulse around me. I take my time leisurely kissing her, showing her with my mouth how much I cherish her.

"Luke," she mumbles against my lips.

"Yeah?" I ask, kissing her again.

"Move."

"Not this time, Addy. This time we're taking things nice and slow." A man of my word, I pull back and then slowly push forward. Over and over, my pace is set. Slow and steady. Her hands are gripping my biceps, her nails digging into my skin. I kiss her, unhurried and deep, just like my thrusts.

"Lucas," she huffs. "There. Please. Don't. Stop," she pants.

Bracing my arms on either side of her head, I focus on keeping my stride, holding off my own orgasm. With each thrust, I feel her spasm around me. I don't need the scream of my name tumbling from her lips to know she's there. I can feel it. Her grip grows tighter, nails dig deeper, and I unleash, thrusting hard and fast before spilling over inside of her.

Drenched in sweat, I pull back, and she whimpers. Falling onto the bed beside her, I gather her in my arms. Neither one of us says anything, because no words are needed. We've declared our love with our bodies and our hearts. The future, our future is in front of us, and I can't wait to see where it takes us. Sluggishly, I drift off to sleep thinking about what comes next.

chapter
twenty-three

Addyson

I'm sitting at my desk staring into space when I should be getting caught up on my charting from my last patient. Instead, I keep thinking about Luke. Last night, we made dinner together at his place. Nothing fancy, just some pasta and a salad, but it was the company that was spectacular. Every day with him I fall even more in love. I swore to myself it would never happen again. I thought if by chance, I were lucky enough to fall in love again, it would be in a few years. I was jaded, but then Luke wormed his way into my heart, and I've never been happier.

It's been a few weeks since I confessed to him that I loved him. I didn't need his words to know he felt the same, but I will admit hearing him tell me gives me a sense of completion I've never felt. When my phone vibrates, I know it's him. He's been texting me all morning. He and Justin and a few of their friends go fishing in Michigan every summer. He's been looking for reasons not to go all weekend.

Lucas: What if you get lonely sleeping all alone?

I can't help but smile.

Me: Oh, Javier is coming over to make sure that doesn't happen.

I giggle. I already know what his reaction is going to be.

Lucas: Addyson!

Lucas: See. I'm staying home.

Lucas: He's not getting his hands on what's mine.

Me: It's already scheduled. I had to pay big money for him too. No refunds.

Lucas: Addyson!

I'm full on laughing now when my phone rings. "Hello," I sputter.

"You're enjoying this," he says.

"Kind of," I admit.

"Do you have any idea what it does to me to think of another man in your bed?"

"Oh, I had planned on staying at your place," I say sweetly.

"Fuck," he mumbles under his breath.

"I'm teasing you. Go hang out with the guys. Have a good time."

"I've never not wanted to go," he admits.

"I'll still be here when you get back."

"Come with us."

"That's a negative. Besides, it's a guys' weekend. Harper and I have plans for movie night and some shopping."

"Fine," he grumbles. "Sunday night… make that Sunday afternoon, those assholes are getting up early so I can get home to you. I'm coming for you," he says huskily.

"I'll be here waiting. I love you. Have a fun, safe trip. Are you headed out now?"

"In a couple of hours. I can swing by and see you," he offers.

"I have a patient still today, and then my own appointment after."

"Right. Okay. Well, I guess I'll see you Sunday."

"It's two days, Luke. Not even two full days. You saw me this morning so it's just tomorrow."

"That's too long." I can hear the humor in his voice, but I know he's being serious.

"Mom's calling me," he says. "We need to meet the parents, babe."

"I agree. Now, have fun. I love you. I'll see you soon."

"I love you, too."

After a couple more goodbyes, we finally end the call. I sit back in my chair still wearing a smile.

"Addyson." The receptionist, Samantha, peeks her head in my office. "Your last patient is here."

Looking at the clock on the wall, I see it's five minutes past the appointment time. The rule is if you're fifteen minutes late you have to reschedule. The majority of my patients are children, who have no control of how or when they get here. This one in particular is usually always punctual. Always, so I'm sure his mom has a good reason. "Thanks, Samantha. Go ahead and put him in a room." I'm leaving early today for a doctor's appointment.

"He's by himself," she counters.

"What? What's going on?" Nolan's mom is always with him.

She shrugs. "Not sure. He walked in on his own, signed himself in and everything."

"Okay." I stand from my chair. "I'm right behind you." This is highly unusual and with his age, I won't be able to treat him today.

"Hi, Miss S." Six-year-old Nolan waves his hand high in the air over his head.

"Mr. Forrester," I greet him, and he giggles. "Where's your mom?"

He shrugs. "My dad bringded me today."

"Your dad brought you today," I correct him. He nods his little head up and down. The mention of his dad surprises me. I've been working with Nolan for almost a year now and not once have I met his father. His mom has mentioned in the past that he's not involved in Nolan's life. He calls every so often and sometimes visits. Only when it's convenient for him. So to hear that he's the one who brought him today and left him no less surprises me.

"My mommy had to wok," he explains.

"Where is your dad?" I ask him.

He shrugs. "Hims said himed drwopeded me off and was calling my mommy."

"Well, let's get started." I give him a bright smile, not letting him know that what his dad did was so incredibly wrong.

"Yo dwess is pwetty, Miss S," he says, climbing into the chair across from my desk.

"Thank you." He truly is such a sweet little boy. All his mother's influence I'm sure. "So tell me what's been going on with you?" I ask him. Part of speech therapy is to get them talking and help correct them when they're speaking.

"Nufing," he says, propping his little arm up on the arm of the chair.

"Nothing." I say the word slowly, and he tries to repeat me. This isn't his first rodeo. "How's school?"

"Good."

Okay, one word answers it is. Usually he's a little chatterbox. I can only assume it's his father's influence. That's the only change that I'm aware of. "Did you get all signed up for baseball?"

"Yeah," he sighs. "I wove football. My unc pways wif me lots."

I smile. This isn't the first time he's mentioned his uncle. I slowly repeat his words back to him. He then tries to sound them out as I've said them. "That's great, Nolan. You know what else?" He shakes his head. "I bet if you asked your uncle, he'd play baseball with you too."

A grin lights up his face. "Hims will," he agrees.

"He will." We spend the next twenty minutes working on sound articulation. Nolan has come a long way with his therapy. When the appointment ends, I walk him out to the waiting room. Nolan rushes ahead of me, and swings open the door. He cheers and then he's gone. When I make it to the door, I see him run to a man who is smiling widely at him. I see him run right into the arms of my boyfriend.

I stand frozen at the door as I watch Nolan jump in his arms and hug him as tight as his little arms will allow.

He has a kid.

But that can't be right.

I search for anything that can explain this, but Nolan's words come back to me. They sit heavily in my stomach.

Luke lied to me.

There must be another explanation. My mind races to find one.

My heart can't accept the fact that he might be like all the others.

I can't deal with this. Seeing Nolan is safe, I step back into the hall and close the door behind me. I'm certain Luke didn't see me as Nolan had all his attention. My legs feel like rubber as I make my way down the hall and back to my office. There's an ache in my chest so profound I feel as though it's been cut open. Hot tears prick my eyes, but I hold them off. Choking back a sob that wants to break free, I stumble into my office and shut the door. As soon as the click of the lock is turned, I lose my battle and the tears begin to fall. I know I need to talk to him. I need to face this, but my head is muddled with what this means. I have an appointment to get to and he's leaving for the weekend. We can talk when he gets back. It will give me time to get my thoughts in order. Prepare myself for the worst and hope for the best.

Pain.

Heartache.

Betrayal.

How could he do this to me? How could I be so blind? Lucas always seemed so open and honest. The way he looks at me... it's as if I'm his world. How could this happen? Did his mom lie to me too? There has to be another explanation for this. Surely, his family knows. What's wrong with me? Why do these things keep happening to me? A million thoughts race through my mind. My phone vibrates on my desk.

Lucas: I miss you already.

I stare at the message. Is this all just a game to him? His insistence that he's going to miss me, that he missed me already. He's with his son, the one he hardly has anything to do with, and he's texting me. He's rushing off to a guys' weekend when he should be spending time with his son. My fingers hover over the screen, poised to send him a message. Instead, I lock my phone and toss it back on my desk. Slumping down in my chair, I bury my face in my hands and try to rein in my emotions. I know what I saw, but I also know there could be a logical explanation. I can't go firing off messages before he leaves to go out of town accusing, not before giving him a chance to explain himself. I've been through this before. I should be used to it. Lucas... he was different. The love I have for him was so much more than any before him.

Grabbing some tissues from the box on my desk, I clean

myself up the best that I can. Closing down my laptop, I pack up my bag and my notes. I'll have to finish charting this weekend. I hate being behind, but right now, I won't be able to wrap my head around any of it. Double-checking I have everything, I throw my purse into my work bag and toss it over my shoulder. I snag my phone and keys from my desk and turn out the light.

"Heading out?" Samantha asks.

"Yeah. I'll see you on Monday."

"Have a great weekend," she says with a bright smile and a wave.

Samantha is always smiling and laughing with the kids. They adore her. I'm lucky that she's my assistant. "You too," I tell her. "You leaving early today?"

"Nah, I'm going to get caught up on some filing and a few other things. Saving my time for the wedding." She holds up her sparkling diamond engagement ring that her long-term boyfriend proposed with a few weeks ago.

"Good plan." I give her a fake smile. I love Samantha. She's worked for me for a couple of years now. I don't begrudge her happiness. I just wish that I could find mine. I keep falling for these guys who are boys. One day, I want to find a man who will love me, honestly and truly. Until then, I need to deal with my current situation. I need to confront him and see what he has to say for himself. I have all weekend to prepare myself for what might be the end of us. Although it's hard, I push it out of my mind and head to my appointment before I'm late.

I'm sitting in the exam room in a thin cotton gown, with an even thinner paper blanket covering my nether regions. The joys of being a woman. I hate these appointments. They're quick but always very uncomfortable. Men don't know how good they have it. They treat us like shit after everything we go through to bring life into the world. Not that I would know anything about that, but the idea is there. I have a monthly cycle, cramps, acne, mood swings, the list goes on and on. All I ask is for someone to love me, to respect me enough for me to be the only woman in their life.

There's a quick knock on the door before Dr. Edwards steps into the room. "Hello, Addyson. How are you?"

"Good," I tell her. "Ready to get this over with."

She chuckles. "You're not the only one. It's a necessary evil of being a woman."

"It's like you read my mind," I mumble.

"What's that?" she asks.

"Nothing. I was just thinking about everything women go through. Men don't realize how easy they have it."

She laughs. "You're not the first to mention that." She takes a seat on her stool and turns to face me. "Okay, let's chat. Anything new since last year? Any pain or discomfort with sex? Discharge?" She goes on to ask a laundry list of embarrassing questions.

"No to all of the above."

"Great. We'll do a quick exam and get your urine results and get you on your way." She types a few things on her computer. "Hmmm. Addyson, it seems that I have some news." She turns to face me.

"O-kay," I say slowly, not sure where she's going with this. We haven't even gotten to the exam yet.

"I know you're here for your yearly exam and birth control refill, and I can do one of those two things. However, your refill I can't do."

"What? Why? Is there something else you recommend?"

"Addyson, you're pregnant."

"I'm sorry. Could you repeat that? I thought you said I was pregnant."

"I did."

"No. No. No. No. I'm on birth control." This cannot be happening. If she would have told me this morning I was pregnant, I would have been shocked, but happy. Now, after learning that Lucas lied to me, after knowing he has hardly anything to do with his son, I can't be.

"Have you been having unprotected sex?" she asks.

"Yes."

She nods. "Nothing is 100 percent effective. Have you been on any medications or under a lot of stress?"

"No." I run through the past few months, and nothing stands out. If anything, I've been happier than I've ever been being with Luke.

"Again, nothing is 100 percent except for abstinence. Is the father in the picture?"

"My boyfriend," I croak. Technically he's still my boyfriend. I'm not sure how true that statement will be after I confront him about what I saw today.

"Addyson, are you all right?" Dr. Edwards asks.

"Y-yes," I say, clearing my throat. "H-how far along? I mean, I don't know when...."

"We can do a vaginal ultrasound today and have a better idea of how far along you are."

I nod. Words escape me. Dr. Edwards tells me she's going to go see if the tech is available and leaves the room. Stepping off the exam table, I grab my phone from my purse and send a text to Harper. We were supposed to meet at her place later, but this can't wait.

Me:	Appointment ended early. Thought I'd stop by and see you.
Harper:	Of course, it's been forever. You can see my new desk.
Me:	Okay. Need anything?

Harper: Nope. I'm off at that time. We can grab a drink in the bar here.

My fingers hover over the screen. I can't tell her over the phone. Hell, I'm not sure I can tell her at all. This is so messed up. Only me. Only my life would turn out to be a damn soap opera.

Me: See you soon.

I leave my reply vague. If I say no to a drink, she's going to know something's up. I don't want that. Not until I decide what to say, how to tell her. And really if I tell anyone first, it should be Luke. He's a lying bastard, but he still deserves to know.

Forty minutes later, I'm walking out of the doctor's office prescription in hand. Only this is not the one I was hoping for. Prenatal vitamins and images of a little black blob are more than I bargained for, but what I got all the same. Dr. Edwards talked to me about choices, but there is only one choice. I'm keeping this baby. I might not ever find a man who will love me, but this baby will. Maybe it will be a little boy. Setting my purse in the passenger seat, I place the pictures and the prescription in the glove box. I'm not ready for anyone to see them. Not yet. After I see Harper and tell her about Luke, I'll have all weekend to figure out what I'm going to say. I need to consider how I'm going to tell him he crushed my heart and gave me one at the same time. Tell him we're over and then oh by the way… you're going to be a father. Again.

chapter
twenty-four

LUCAS

I've checked my phone at least a hundred times today. I texted Addy a couple of hours ago and still haven't heard back from her. That's not normal for her. My gut tells me that something's wrong.

"So what was the deal with Nolan?" Justin asks.

"Fuck, can we not go there? I can't deal with that drama and Addy ignoring me." I check my phone again; it's been a whole thirty seconds.

"Luke, man, can you put that thing away?" Nick says, twisting the top off another beer.

It's late, a little past midnight, and we just got to the house on Lake Michigan that we rented for the weekend. Well, now that we're older, it's more of one day of fishing. Adulting's a bitch. I take one more glance at my phone then slide it into my pocket.

"She still not get back to you?" Trevor asks.

"Nope."

"Harper said they had dinner and a few drinks. She's at her place," Justin tells me.

I'm glad to know she's safe, but that still doesn't explain why she's ghosted me.

"Chill out." Nick chuckles. "Your girl will be there when you get back. Unless of course, she's already moved on to someone else. What was his name? Javier?" He laughs.

It's my fault. I made the mistake of rambling about our earlier phone call when I couldn't get hold of her. I knew better with this group, but I don't give a shit what they dish out. I'm worried about her. This isn't like her, so of course I'm going to worry. About a half an hour later, we've finished our beers and head off to bed. We have an early day tomorrow and a long one at that. Settling in my room, I send her another message.

Me: Goodnight, Addy. I love you.

If she's been drinking, I'm sure she's out for the night, but she'll see it when she wakes up. She'll know I was thinking about her.

I'm always thinking about her.

The next morning we're up and out of the house by six. I don't expect her to be up this early, but I fire off another message anyway.

Me: Morning, beautiful. Headed out on the lake. Love you.

I keep it simple. I'm well aware I'm freaking out. It's new to me, this longing that I have for her. This deep-seated need to know that she's okay. Not knowing how she is, not hearing from her, it's hard. As in, my heart can't take it.

"Put the damn phone down," Nick grumbles. "Give the girl some room to breathe."

"She's breathing just fine." I look over at Justin and he nods.

"Harper says she's still sleeping."

I sigh. She's okay. That alone has my anxiety simmering, but it still doesn't explain why she's not returning my messages. "Thanks," I croak.

"She's got her hooks in you, huh?" Trevor asks, holding up a big-ass fishing hook.

"Yep." I don't bother denying it. I'm not ashamed of Addyson or how I feel about her. In fact, it's the opposite. I want to shout it to the world that she's mine.

The day drags on with me checking my phone incessantly. Still nothing from Addyson. Justin talked to Harper, and she told him they were headed out to go shopping for the day. That has been their plan. However, she's still not responding to me. I know she's okay, so now I'm getting pissed off. Why is she ghosting me? We talked earlier yesterday and everything was fine. We were laughing and joking; she told me she loved me. Now it's crickets. Not a single reply, not even a fucking thumbs-up.

"Did Harper say anything?" I ask Justin.

"No, just that Addy had a bad day yesterday and she needed some retail therapy."

"What? What happened? Can you call her and ask her?"

He's already shaking his head. "No can do, brother. Harper already asked me not to ask her because she didn't want to lie to me, and she promised Addy she wouldn't say anything."

"What the fuck?" I toss my half-eaten lunchmeat sandwich into the lake. My appetite is long gone. "I don't get it," I tell him. "We were fine. What could have happened between our phone call and a few hours?"

"I'm not sure, and Harper is tight-lipped."

"Damn it." Leaning forward in my chair, I rest my elbows on my knees and bury my hands in my hair.

"Are you really going to let some pussy get you down like

this?" Trevor asks.

"That pussy is my fucking girlfriend," I say. He can tell by my tone that he's pissed me off, but that doesn't stop him.

"You sure about that?" he contests.

"Yeah, how long have you known this one anyway? Is her pussy made of gold or something? She's got you all up in knots."

"A few months, and we" — I motion at my chest and then to where they're sitting across from Justin and me — "are never talking about her pussy."

Trevor raises his hands in defeat. "Just some food for thought, brother."

"You don't know her."

"Do you?" Nick challenges.

Do I know her? "Hell, yes I do." I know that her hair feels like silk. I know that when I kiss just below her ear, it drives her crazy. I know that her favorite color is teal, and she loves her cowboy boots. I know that she's been hurt and that her heart is hesitant to trust. I know that my heart is hers. There isn't a single doubt in my mind. So, yeah, I know her.

"Well, nothing you can do about it now. If she's not answering your calls or messages you just have to wait until we get back into town," Nick says.

Waiting.

I hate waiting.

My heart can't take it. The worry that she's changed her mind, that something I've said has spooked her... it's the only explanation. Pulling my phone out of my pocket, I swipe across the screen, and still nothing. I fire off another text.

Me: I love you, Addy. I don't know what's going on, but when I get home tomorrow,

I'm coming to you. Whatever it is, we'll get through it together. Please talk to me.

Me: Please, baby.

Just as I'm putting my phone back in my pocket, it pings with a text. Everyone stops, all four of us as I look at the message.

Addyson: Text me when you are back in town. We need to talk.

"What's it say?" Justin asks.

I read off the message and Trevor whistles. "Doesn't sound good."

He's right. I have no idea what could have happened, but what I do know is that she's in for a fight. I'm not giving up on us, not letting her go that easily.

Me: Your place or mine?

Addyson: Mine.

Me: I'll come straight there.

I wait for her reply and get nothing. I want to tell the guys we're packing up and heading home tonight, but I need to take some time to cool off. I'm pissed that she's keeping me in the dark. Going to her now, with anger fresh in my veins, isn't a good idea. We'll both say things we'll regret. My end game is to keep her, to make her my wife. Going in attitude blazing will not get me there. Of that I'm certain.

The entire drive home I kept my phone in my hand. I was hoping to hear from her, but I should have known better. About an hour away, I texted her letting her know I was on my way. I didn't get a reply, but she's expecting me, and if she's not there, that's fine. I'll wait. We're getting to the bottom of this today.

Pulling into her drive, I don't see her car. I park my truck and thrum my fingers against the steering wheel, trying to stay calm. I'm still pissed off that she's kept me in the dark, but the fear that something is going on with her, something real... like her doctor gave her bad news, that fear is palpable and overrides my anger. I just need to lay eyes on her, hold her, and assure her that no matter what it is, we've got this.

Together, we've got this.

Me: I'm at your place.

I stare at my phone willing her to reply. Minutes tick by with nothing. Where could she be? I turn on the radio to a local station to see if they mention any kind of accidents. My gut twists at the thought of something happening to her. Finally, after five long agonizing minutes, my phone alerts me to a text.

Addyson: Be there in five.

Dread. That's what I feel. Dread. Never in my life has a woman told me we should talk and it ended on a good note. I'm not letting her walk away from me, though. We've come too far, my love too deep to just watch her go.

Me: Be safe.

Addyson: K.

I scan through the radio stations, but nothing holds my interest. Nothing but the rearview mirror as I watch for her to pull into her driveway seems to gain my attention. My mind races with what we need to talk about. If it's not us, then what? Is she sick? Is she hurt? My heart seems to fall to the pit of my stomach. Whatever it is, I'll fix it. I will do everything in my power to make it better. No way am I losing her. Not now that I've finally found her.

Finally, I see her car, and I'm out of my truck and waiting to open her door for her. She's visibly upset, and if the puffy redness of her eyes is any indication, she's been crying. I don't ask her what's wrong. I don't say a word. I simply open her door, and when she steps out of the car, I pull her into my body, hugging her tightly, silently praying that whatever it is, whatever she has to tell me, whatever news she has doesn't take her away from me.

"We should go inside," she says, pushing away.

I reach for her hand, but she pulls away. Instead of

questioning her, I follow behind like the lovesick fool I am. Inside her condo, she sets her things down on the entryway table, her bags on the floor, and makes her way into the living room. She reaches for a small white envelope on the table. Is it test results? My imagination is running wild with what could be in that little white package that has my girl so upset. I want to insist she tell me now, that she tell me what the news is so I can hold her. I'll hold her all night and then tomorrow morning. I'll hold her through whatever it is that has her so visibly upset. She won't do this alone. I'll make damn sure of it.

"Have a seat," she says, curling her legs under her in the chair. It's a deliberate move as I'll have to sit on the couch. Away from her. "Today's been an off day."

"I can see that you're upset. Can I hold you? I don't care what it is. We'll get through it. Together."

"What exactly do you think is going on here, Lucas?"

"I assume something happened at the doctor's on Friday. That you got bad news or something?"

She nods. "News, but it's not bad. At least, I don't think so. I was shocked at first, but it's not something I can be upset about."

I feel as though a ton of bricks has been lifted off my chest. She's going to be okay. That's all that matters. "Want to talk about it?"

"Not really, but that's not the adult thing to do." She pauses, collecting her thoughts I assume so I remain quiet, giving her the time that she needs. "I saw you Friday afternoon, when you were at my office."

"You did? I was hoping to see you while I was there. I didn't see you when I was in the lobby, and I had to get back. The guys were ready and waiting on me."

"Right," she scoffs. "Please stop with the lies, Lucas."

What? "I'm not lying to you. I hoped to get to see you. Hell, if I had it my way, I'd spend every waking moment with you."

"And your son?"

"My son?" I ask, puzzled.

"The one you've kept hidden from me. The one you hardly have anything to do with. What about him?"

"Addyson? What the hell are you talking about?"

"You ready to hear my news?" she asks, ignoring my question.

"Yes." We can go back to the fact that she thinks I have a son. I don't know where she would get that idea.

"I'm pregnant."

It takes about three seconds for what she's saying to sink in. Slowly, I stand and walk to where she's sitting on the chair. I drop to my knees and place my hand on her belly. Tears prick my eyes.

Holy shit. I'm going to be a father.

"A baby," I whisper. Lifting my head, my watery eyes collide with hers. "I love you, Addy. We made a baby." I can't contain my smile. Not that I want to.

"It appears that way," she says, wiping her cheeks.

"You're happy about it, that's what you said, but you don't look happy." She looks pained if the sorrow in her tear-filled eyes is any indication.

"Happy that the man I love has been lying to me. That you skimp out on your responsibilities as a father now, how could I possibly think that this baby, that our baby will be any different?"

"What the fuck are you talking about?" I can feel the anger set in. This is the best fucking day of my life, and she's coming off with this random "you have a kid" bullshit. "Please stop talking in circles and tell me what's going on."

"Nolan." Her voice breaks. "He's an amazing little boy. You're missing out on that. On him."

"Nolan?" I ask, confused. That's when it hits me. "Addyson, Nolan is my nephew."

"Yeah, okay." She laughs humorlessly. "Are you really going to lie to my face? I saw you, Lucas. He even looks like you. He said his dad dropped him off. His dad that his mom, Annalyse, claims is not in his life."

I stand up and reach for her hand, pulling her out of the chair. I then take the seat where she was sitting and pull her into my lap. She doesn't fight me on it, but she's stiff in my arms. "Listen to me," I say, my lips next to her ear. "Nolan Oliver Forrester is my nephew. Annalyse Forrester is my sister. Kirk, that's Nolan's dad, he dropped him off and left. He called my sister at work telling her she had to deal with it." She's still stiff, but she's not moving. "She called me asking if I would be able to pick him up and meet her at her place. She was in a meeting she couldn't leave." Still nothing so I keep going. "I don't have a son, not unless this little one is a boy. And for the record, I don't have a daughter either." I wait patiently, my arms holding her close for her to speak.

"How am I supposed to believe you? He said his dad dropped him off, and you were there, and I've never seen you there before. You never called him Nolan," she says. Her voice is sad, almost like she's not fighting me. No, it's more like she's accepted it.

"My father's middle name is Oliver, just like mine and Nolan's. We've called him Ollie since he was a baby," I explain. "I didn't even put two and two together that you were Ollie's speech therapist until Anna gave me the address. She's never mentioned you by name, instead referring to you as his speech therapist, or Miss S. I should have asked, but it never occurred to me."

That's when I feel her entire body start to tremble.

"Shh, please don't cry. It's not good for you or for the baby." She burrows into my chest. "It's okay," I assure her.

"No," she sobs. "It's not okay, Luke. It's all too much."

"What's too much?" I ask gently. I'm trying to remain calm.

Is having my baby too much? She said she was excited, but now with the tears, I'm at a loss.

She sits up, then stands and walks across the room. Her arms are crossed tightly across her chest. "This, it's all too much. You say he's your nephew, and I have no reason to not believe you. I immediately thought the worst of you. I'm broken, and you deserve better."

"What I deserve is you," I say. I fight the urge to go to her, but I grip the arms of the chair and stay where I am, giving her the space she's seeking.

"Right," she scoffs. "You need a girlfriend who jumps to conclusions. Shit, I'm going to screw this baby up."

I stand, and in a few long strides, I'm standing before her. "Listen to me. You've been through so much, and I know what those other assholes put you through. It was a misunderstanding. No harm done. However, don't you ever talk about the mother of my child that way." I step closer, raising my hands to wipe the tears from her cheeks. "She's beautiful and kind. She's wicked smart and loyal. She's my best friend and my heart."

"Luke," she breathes, tears falling down her cheeks.

"I once told her I would prove to her that I'm the difference. That I wouldn't treat her as those before me had. That I would make it my mission in life to be what she needs. You know what the funny part of that is?"

She shakes her head. "No," she whispers.

I drop to my knees and place my hand under her shirt over her belly. Looking up, I see her big brown eyes wet from tears but full of hope. "I wanted to be your difference, but it turns out you're mine. You and our baby."

"I'm so sorry," she cries.

"You have nothing to be sorry for. Come here." I stand back up and guide her to the couch. I sit, and she snuggles in next to me.

"I've made a mess of things."

"No, you haven't. This is our first fight. I'm sure it won't be our last. What you have to remember is that I'd rather fight with you, than be without you. We're a family."

She sits up and turns to face me. "I have pictures." She reaches out and snags the white envelope she was holding when I got here off the coffee table. "You can't really tell, but it's his or her first pictures." She smiles through her tears.

My hands tremble as I take the envelope from her. Carefully, I pull out the black and white photos. "Baby, I need some help. What am I looking at here?"

"This — " She points to a small black blob. " — is our baby."

"Did you know?" I ask her. I stare at the grainy image trying to process that the little black blob is making me a father.

"No." She shakes her head. "No clue. Friday was my yearly checkup and refill on my birth control. They always do a urine pregnancy test and it came back positive."

"Shocked?" I ask her. I was initially as well, but the shock was quickly replaced with elation. I love this woman, and our baby. How could I not be happy about that?

"Very. But after a few minutes, the shock wore off and it was more sadness. I thought I was going to be doing this alone. And I can, I can do this alone."

"I know you can, but you won't be." I lean over and kiss her lips. "This is our baby, and we'll be raising her together."

"Her?"

"Yep. I hope it's a little girl who looks just like her momma."

"Healthy. I just want him or her to be healthy."

"Move in with me."

"What?" She pulls back, shock evident on her face.

"Move in with me. I love you. I love this baby. If I had my way, I would have already moved you in. Let's make it official."

"Luke, you should think about what you're saying."

"I don't need to think about it. I want you there. I don't want to miss a minute of this. Not the pregnancy or the late-night feedings. I want all of it. I want all of you."

She's quiet for a few minutes. "You really are the difference."

"Damn right I am. So, move in with me?" This time it's posed as more of a question. She bites down on her bottom lip. "My house is a home with you there. Now, with this little angel joining us, even more so. We can keep this place for a few months if that makes you feel better," I offer. I'm grasping at straws to get her to say yes. I'm just about to tell her I'll sign my house over to her, so she always has a place to call home when my phone rings. Pulling it out of my pocket, I see Anna's name. I turn it so that Addy can see before answering.

"Unc Luke," Ollie or Nolan, as Addy knows him, says into the phone.

"You coming to mammy's?" he asks.

"Hey, bud. I'm not sure. Let me talk to your mom, okay?"

"'Kay," he says. I can hear rustling then my sister's amused voice.

"Sorry about that. His speech therapist told him you would throw the baseball with him."

"Oh, she did, did she?" I ask, smiling to myself. Just wait until she finds out Miss S is my Addyson.

"Yes, but you don't have to. I know you just got in. We're at Mom and Dad's for dinner."

"You know what, count me in. I have someone I want you to meet."

"Really? You're finally going to let us meet her?"

"Your future sister-in-law, yes."

"What? You're engaged?" she screeches.

"No. Not yet, but I'm going to be, and it's going to be her."

"Yes! I can't wait to meet her."

"See you soon," I say, ending the call not waiting for her

reply. "So, we need to swing by my parents' house."

"Now?" she asks. "And future sister-in-law?"

"Yes, now. Ollie said his speech therapist told him I would throw the baseball with him. And well, since his dad is a deadbeat, I want to. I also want you to finally meet my family. It's long overdue." I lean in and kiss her. "And yes, Addyson, you are my future. My future wife, my forever."

"I'm a mess, Luke, and... don't we need to talk about all that?"

"Nope. You know where I stand. I want you and the baby to move in with me. Tonight. However, I know you need some time to process it all so we can start moving you in tomorrow."

"Tomorrow?" She smiles. "Thanks for the time to process."

"You're welcome." I kiss the tip of her nose.

"I'm sorry," she says sincerely. "I shouldn't have jumped to conclusions without talking to you first."

"It's okay, baby. I get it. Now, up. Ollie's waiting on me." After she takes a minute to "clean up," as she put it, I snake an arm around her shoulders and lead her out to my truck. After all the worry over the past couple of days, I couldn't have asked for a better outcome. Sure, I'm hurt she didn't trust me, but I get it. She's been shit on more times than she can count. Life is full of pain without forgiveness. There is nothing I want more than her and our baby. As far as I'm concerned, it's all water under the bridge. Today we start the next chapter of our life. As parents, if I have my way married parents. I just have to take it one step at a time.

chapter
twenty-five

Addyson

Once we're on the road, Luke reaches over and takes my hand in his, resting them on the center console. I'm in awe of him and his understanding. He should be pissed off, raging mad, but instead, he's grinning like a fool. He's happy about the baby and wants us to be a family. It's more than I could have hoped, but I know that's all on me. I let my past and my insecurities take over. I accused him when I should have stepped out into that waiting room and dealt with it head-on. Instead, I pulled into my shell. I expected him to walk, not insist I move in with him.

"Do you want to tell them about the baby?" he asks, breaking into my thoughts.

"Do you?"

"Hell yes, I do. I just know some people wait, right? Morgan from the office, she waited until she was at a certain point in her pregnancy before telling anyone."

"Yeah, I know some do, but… it's your family, you can tell them if you want."

"They are my family, but you and our baby, you're my family too and my first priority."

"It's your call."

"Have you told your parents?"

"No. Not even Harper."

"Really?" He glances over, and I can hear the surprise in his voice.

"No, just told her that you're not who I thought you were. That you had a son. I guess I should call her and tell her, huh?"

"Nah, she'll spill to Justin I'm sure. He can set her straight. If not, we can later. Right now, you're meeting my family." He pulls into a circular drive. "This is my parents' place." He turns his truck off and faces me. "We can tell them or not tell them, but before we go in there, I need you to convey to me that you understand something. I need to hear you say to me that you know I'm in this. That I love you and this baby, and I want you both."

"You love me and our baby," I say, fighting a smile. "I'm sorry, Lucas, for everything."

"You moving in with me?"

I want to. I want that trust that we built, I want it to continue to grow, and I want this baby to have both of his or her parents. "Yes." I don't give myself time to second-guess my answer. I'm following my heart and this time, I trust Luke will be there to protect it.

"Yeah?" He leans over the console, snakes his hand around the back of my neck, and pulls me into a kiss. "I love you so fucking much." He rests his forehead against mine.

"I love you too." I hear a squeal and look up to find Nolan rushing out of the house. "Looks like he's excited."

"He's a great kid."

I nod. "I know."

"Come on, let's go meet your future in-laws." I smile nervously, but he doesn't see it. He also doesn't see the way my heart flutters in my chest. He's already out of the truck and headed to my side. He opens the door for me and lifts me to the ground. "Precious cargo," he says, kissing the tip of my nose before setting me on my feet.

We hear a gasp. Together we turn to look at Nolan. He's standing with his hands on his hips, and his little head tilted to the side. "What's yous doing kissing Miss S?" he asks Luke. You can tell from his face he's truly perplexed.

Luke bends so they are eye-to-eye. "Want to know something cool?" he asks his nephew. He bobs his little head up and down. "Miss S is my girlfriend."

"Dos shes have cooties?" he asks.

Luke chuckles. "No, but you know what she does have?" he asks him. This time Nolan shakes his head from side to side. "She has a baby in her belly." Luke reaches up and entwines his fingers with mine.

"Yous do?" Nolan asks wide-eyed.

"I do," I confirm with a smile.

"Come on, buddy, let's go inside for a few minutes and then we can play catch."

"Miss S pway too?"

"Not this time, little man." Luke stands.

"Why not?" I ask him.

"Yeah, whys not?" Nolan says, standing next to her.

"The baby," Luke says softly.

"Luke, I'm pregnant not injured. I can toss the ball with him."

"What if the ball hits you? In the belly," he adds.

"He's six," I remind him. "I don't think we have to worry about that."

"Not this time, okay?" he asks, kissing my temple.

"Is this what the next eight months are going to be? You telling me what I can and can't do?"

"Probably." He shrugs unapologetically. "That's my job, to take care of you and this baby."

"No, your job is to love us."

"I do, Addy."

"I know you do. Come on. We can talk about this later." I nod toward where Nolan is staring up at us.

"I's not hurt yous baby, Miss S."

"Oh, sweetheart." I bend down to get close to him. "I know you won't. In fact, you're going to be a big cousin. You're going to need to teach the baby how to run and play, and all kinds of other fun stuff."

"Yay!" He throws his little arms up in the air.

"All right, bud. We'll be back out in a few. Stay in the yard and don't go past the trees." Luke points to the tree line that's midway through the yard.

"I's won't," he says, skipping off to play.

"Ready?" Luke smiles down at me.

"As I'll ever be." He leads us toward the front of the house. When we get close, the door opens, and a woman who has to be his mother with salt-and-pepper hair greets us.

"It's about time." She gives Luke a mock glare then turns to me. "You must be the woman my son can't stop talking about."

"Addyson," I say, holding out my hand.

"Pft." She bypasses my hand and pulls me into a hug. "He told his sister you were her future sister-in-law. That deserves a hug," she says, pulling away.

"It's a pleasure to meet you," I say, avoiding the sister-in-law bit. I'm overwhelmed with how accepting they are of mine and Luke's declaration.

"Mom, this is my girlfriend, Addyson. Addy, this is my mother, Gail. Where's Dad?"

"In the house with Anna. Come on in." She steps back to let us through, calling out to Nolan telling him to not pass the trees.

"Yo, Pops," Luke calls.

"We're in here." I recognize Annalyse's voice right away. With his arm around my waist, Luke guides us into the kitchen. His father looks up and smiles, as does his sister. She gasps. "Addyson! This is your Addyson?" she asks Luke.

"No, Mommy. This is my Miss S," Nolan says from behind us. We all turn to look at him. He has dirt on his face, but his smile is blinding. He stops to stand next to me. "Hers gots a baby in hers belly, and Imma teach it to run and stuff." I wait for the dread to hit me that our news has been leaked, but it never comes. I want this baby, and I'm proud to be sharing this experience with Luke.

"Luke?" his mom asks. Her hand flies over her mouth and tears well in her eyes. I watch as his father stands and goes to her, pulling her into his arms. It's as if we're looking in a mirror when Luke does the same thing to me.

"Looks like the cat's out of the bag." Luke smiles down at me. "We're having a baby," he says, his voice loud and clear, his eyes soft and only for me.

Before I know what's happening, there are four sets of arms wrapped around us in a hug. All the adults are talking at once until we hear a gasp. Everyone pulls away to see Nolan gripping my legs. "I's was stuck," he says, shrugging, causing all of the adults to laugh.

"When are you due?" Anna asks. "How are you feeling?"

"We just found out," Luke says. "We're four weeks and three days." I'm impressed he tacked on the three days from the four weeks and one day on the ultrasound picture.

"I feel great. I wouldn't have known had I not gone in for a checkup."

"I had a great pregnancy with both of my kids. No morning sickness, but I did crave chocolate ice cream and plain potato chips." His mom laughs.

"No cravings yet, but I'm ready for them," Luke says proudly.

"Well, come on in, so we can chat. Let's get comfortable. I'm Phillip, by the way." His dad opens his arms for a hug. I slowly step into them, and he whispers, "Welcome to the family."

That's the moment that it hits me. This has always been my dream. To fall in love and have a family of my own. My parents were such great role models, I wanted my future to look like theirs. Happily in love, watching my kids grow up with my husband beside me every step of the way. I thought that dream had vanished with all of the frogs of my past. Luckily for me, my prince came along and wouldn't take no for an answer.

Luke has made my dreams come true.

We spend the next few hours talking and getting to know each other. Luke goes outside to toss the ball with Nolan. His dad tags along, leaving us women to chat. It helped already knowing Anna, sure in a professional manner, but it was enough to ease my nerves.

"Addy, you about ready to go?" Luke asks sometime later. He's standing in the doorway of the living room. "We have to get you something to eat."

"Stay for dinner," his mom urges.

"Thanks, Mom, but I've been away from my girl since Friday morning. We need some downtime."

"Uh-huh." His sister laughs.

"That too." Luke grins.

"Lucas Oliver Prescott!" his mother scolds him.

"Love you, Mom." He grins, taking my hand and guiding me down the hall. "We'll call you," he calls over his shoulder as we reach the door. He doesn't wait for an answer as we step out and close it behind us.

"I meant what I said, but you think we should go see your parents?" he asks once we're in his truck.

"Not tonight. I'll call Mom, and maybe we can go over tomorrow night. Right now, I really just want you."

"You need anything from your place?"

"Yeah, I need my bag. It has my laptop in it."

He pulls our joined hands to his lips and kisses my knuckles. "Which room do you think we should decorate for the baby?" he asks, turning off his parents' street.

"Umm... I'm not sure. I think for a few weeks or so, he or she will need to be in the room with us."

"Okay, so we need two beds?" he asks.

"No, a bassinet would work."

"Got it."

"Luke." I wait until we are at a stop sign and he turns to look at me. "We have time."

"I know that, but I want to build a home with you, build our life. I can't help but be excited about this. I mean it, Addy. I want this baby. I couldn't be happier."

I nod. What else can I say? He forgave me for being a fool. I know how lucky I am, and I vow never to jump to conclusions again.

At my place, I rush down the hall to my room to grab my laptop when an idea hits me. In the closet, I pull out my two suitcases. One is larger, the other is small for carry-on purposes. Opening them up, I start tossing in clothes. I empty out the drawer for my bras and panties and socks. I grab a couple pair of night clothes, a few outfits for this week, some shorts, T-shirts, and jeans. I'm tossing in random items until I have the large suitcase full.

In the smaller case, I grab the picture of Luke and me, as well as the one of my parents from the nightstand and wrap them in a towel, placing them gently in the second suitcase. Then I take the framed ultrasound picture from the top of my dresser. It too is wrapped in a towel and placed in the second case. Going back to my closet, I grab my brown and teal cowboy boots and add them before zipping it closed.

"What are you doing?" Luke asks as I'm setting the smaller case on the floor.

"Thought I'd get a head start." I shrug.

"Head start on what?" he asks. I can hear the hope in his voice.

"I thought I was moving in?"

"Yes." He stalks toward me. He picks up both bags and leaves the room.

"What are you doing?" I call after him.

"Not giving you a chance to change your mind. I'll be in the truck."

With a grin on my face a mile wide, I gather my laptop, and just for the smile I know he'll give me when he sees it, I pack another smaller bag. This time, I toss in more casual clothes. When it's full, I zip it up and head to the living room. I grab my favorite blanket from the back of the couch and toss it over my shoulder with my overnight bag and work bag. Turning off the lights, and locking up, I make my way to the truck.

"More?" His eyes light up. He leans down and kisses me softly. "Best day of my life," he whispers against my lips.

"Yeah?"

He nods. "Definitely."

"Want to know a secret?"

"Yours? Of course."

"I want a little boy. I want a little boy who will grow up to be an amazing man just like his father."

"Well, you can have your boy after I get my girl."

"How many?" I ask him.

"As many as you'll give me." He takes my bags and loads them while I take my seat and buckle my seat belt.

"We should call Justin and Harper."

"We can do that when we get home," I tell him.

"Home. Fuck do I like the sound of that. You calling my address home."

"We share an address now, buddy."

"Thank fuck," he says, and we both laugh.

He dials the phone, and we put Justin and Harper on speaker. They're both shocked and happy for us all at the same time. They then drop the news on us that they too are living together. They made it official today as well. Neither one of them liked being away from the other, and they thought it was time.

"You got some catching up to do, man," Luke chides Justin.

"Hear that, Harp? Toss out those pills," he tells her.

She shocks us all when she says. "Okay."

"What?" he asks her. Luke and I are as quiet as mice as we listen.

"I said okay," she says. There's no hesitation in her voice.

"Guys, we're going to go," I tell them, letting them have this moment. They'll be sure to fill us in later. "Love you both," I say, and end the call before they can reply. They're not worried about us right now anyway. There are some big decisions being made all around us. As we lie together in bed, his arms holding me close, I can't help but feel hopeful for our future. Luke has brought so much to my life, and now with our baby on the way, that joy is heightened even further. It takes me a while to fall asleep from all the excitement and changes in our lives, but I'm excited and hopeful that there are many more to come.

chapter
twenty-six

LUCAS

"Does your dad own a gun?" I ask Addy. It's Monday night, and we're on the way to her parents' house.

"He does."

"Great," I mutter.

"What's going on in that head of yours?" she asks.

"Just thinking about our daughter. I'm gonna need to get a gun," I admit.

She chuckles. "Why?"

"Because with a little girl, I have to worry about a million little dicks trying to get into her pants."

"Why do they have to be little?" She smirks.

"Addyson," I say, warning her.

She throws her head back and laughs, the sound filling the cab of my truck. "What if it's a boy?"

"Then I only have to worry about one dick. One big dick, you know since he's taking after his dad and all."

She just shakes her head and grins. "Why didn't you tell me you were nervous?"

"I'm not, not really. I was just thinking about if we have a little girl and how I'll handle a man coming into her life and taking her away from me."

"You'll have to let her make her own choices. As long as he treats her right, that's all we can ask for."

"I guess. You think that's how your dad looks at it?"

"Absolutely. You have nothing to worry about. They'll worry because of my past, but when they see us together, they'll know."

"Yeah? And how's that?"

"Because none of them ever looked at me the way that you do."

"Like I need you next to me to breathe?" It's not an exaggeration. When I'm not with her, I want to be, and I'm constantly worried about her, about the baby. Is she feeling okay? Is she over doing it? She's my entire world.

"Something like that." She agrees with a grin. "Take a left up here. It's the second driveway on the right."

"This the house you grew up in?" I ask when we pull in.

"Yes. Just me and my parents. I always wanted siblings. Mom and Dad said I was enough for them."

"We're having more, right? Not just this one?" She was vague the last time we discussed this.

"How many more?" she asks me.

"At least four in total."

"We'll be out of bedrooms." I love that she's embraced us living together. I thought for sure that I would have a fight on my hands.

"I'm an architect. We can add on."

"Let's start with this one, and maybe one more and see how it goes."

"Deal." I would be happy with one, but I'll take as many as she'll give me. "So we don't have Nolan here to help us out," I say with a chuckle. My nephew is one of a kind.

"No, we don't. They're great. It's going to be fine."

"Regardless, we're happening."

"Yes." She's quick to agree. I'm not nervous for me, but for her. I don't need their permission to love Addy and our baby, but I know it will mean a lot to her. That's why I'm nervous. We've talked about our families, and from what I've heard, they're great, but you never know how people are going to react. Especially since she's their only child.

"Stay put," I tell her, turning off the engine. Surprisingly, she listens. I lean in and kiss the corner of her mouth. "Ready, baby?"

"Yes."

Lifting her from the truck a moment later, I set her on her feet. "Luke, I can manage," she tells me, and it's not the first time.

"Precious cargo." I wink. Her big brown eyes sparkle with happiness.

"Come on, crazy man." She laces her fingers through mine, and we head to the front door. She doesn't knock. Instead, she turns the handle and walks on in. "Mom, Dad, where are you?" she calls.

"In the kitchen, Addy," a masculine voice responds.

She leads us down the hall to a large kitchen. "Hey." She releases my hand and hugs her mom and then her dad. "Mom, Dad, I'd like you to meet Lucas. My boyfriend. Luke, this is my dad, Arthur, and my mom, Barbara."

"It's nice to meet you." I hold my hand out for her father, giving his hand a firm shake, and then to her mom, who much like my own, swats it away and pulls me into a hug.

"It's so nice to finally meet you. Sit." She points to the large dining table off to the side of the kitchen. "I hope you're hungry. I made chicken pot pie, and we have salad."

"That sounds delicious." It smells delicious too.

"We have a few minutes," her mom says.

"That's good because I have some news," Addyson says. I pull her chair out for her and drop a kiss to the top of her head before taking the one next to her. Her hand finds mine underneath the table, and I give it a gentle squeeze in silent support. "Luke and I have decided to move in together."

"You're a big girl, Addyson," her father says. His eyes are soft as he looks at her. "As long as this is what you want, we support you."

She turns to look at me. "He's what I want."

I don't give a shit whose kitchen we're in. I tuck a loose strand of hair behind her ear, and lean in, kissing the corner of her mouth. She smiles up at me, and I swear my fucking heart is smiling with how much I love this woman.

"We have more news. We're having a baby."

Her mother stands and rushes to us, pulling us into a hug. "Congratulations."

"Addyson," her dad says. His eyes are locked on hers. He opens his mouth to speak, but I beat him to it.

"When I met Addy, she told me about all the hell she'd been through. The losers who used her. I can assure you, I'm not those men. I love your daughter, and our baby very much."

He nods. "Addyson tells me you're an architect."

"Yes, sir. I designed our home," I tell him. "We'd love to have you over so you can see it. See where we're going to be raising our family." My eyes stray back to Addyson.

He nods. "Are you happy, Addy?"

"Yes." Her voice is loud and clear. No hesitation.

"That's all I can ask for. You tell us when and we'll be there."

He makes his way toward us and pulls her into a hug.

She pulls out her phone. "I'll text you both our new address so you have it."

"You're welcome anytime," I add.

"How are you feeling?" her mom asks.

"Great. I can't even tell I'm pregnant."

"How far along are you?"

"Four weeks and four days," I say, leaning over and placing my hand on her still flat belly.

"I didn't realize this would be a celebration dinner."

"Mom, it's not a big deal."

"Addyson, you're making us grandparents, this is a very big deal," her dad chimes in.

"Yeah," she agrees. She looks over at me, and I see so much in her eyes. Love is present and shining brightly, as bright as the future we have ahead of us.

I have the ring that I bought today when I left work early. I had planned on showing it to her father, and asking his permission to marry her, but fuck it.

"Mr. and Mrs. Stafford, I know this is unusual, and not at all how I planned it. However, it feels right." Scooting back from the table, I turn her chair to face me and drop to one knee. "Addyson Grace Stafford, you are the love of my life. The moment I laid eyes on you I knew that you were special. I didn't know how, and I didn't know the way you would complete me, but you have in so many ways." I reach up and touch her still flat belly. "There is just one missing piece to our puzzle." I reach into my pocket and pull out the ring box. I don't know if her parents are pissed, and if I could see past their daughter, the beautiful woman beside me, I might chance a look. I don't. All I see is her.

"I love you, Addy. Not because you're having my baby. Not because it's by society's standards the right thing to do. I love you because of your smile. Those big brown eyes that show me the depth of your love every time you look at me. I love your heart and the way you give it so freely. I love our late-night talks. I love coming home to you, love waking up with you. I love the life we have planned, and you would make me the luckiest man on this earth if you would agree to be my wife. Addyson, will you marry me?"

She's nodding before I even finish asking. Tears spill over her cheeks.

"Words, Addyson," her mom says.

"Yes." She smiles, leaning in for a kiss.

I move back to my seat and pull her into my lap. My arms wrap around her waist, and I bury my face in her neck. Her dad clears his throat. I look up to find his eyes on us. "I'm sorry, sir. I know I should have asked for your permission, but I couldn't wait. I want nothing more than to live the rest of my life loving her. I hope you'll both give us your blessing."

Her mom nods, wiping tears from her cheeks.

"Take care of them," he says, surprising me. His face breaks out into a grin. "I could tell it was an 'in the moment' situation."

"Yes, sir. I brought the ring hoping to show you to get some time with you alone, but when it comes to your daughter, I'm not very patient."

"Who does that remind you of?" her mom asks him.

"Us, oh, thirty or so years ago."

"Exactly. Now, let's eat, and we can get to know our future son-in-law." Her mom stands and I offer to help, but she waves me off.

"I'll go." Addyson kisses my cheek, then stands from her seat on my lap, and follows after her mom.

"I've never seen her this happy."

"Good. That's all I want for her."

"I believe you." He reaches across the table and offers me his hand. "Welcome to the family, Lucas. Take care of them," he repeats his earlier words.

"With everything I am," I confirm.

Dinner is delicious, and Addy's parents are just as nice as she described them to be. I'm not so sure I'll be the same laidback parent if our daughter shows up with a boyfriend I've never met, tells me she's pregnant, and then I watch him propose without talking to me first. I'm lucky Arthur didn't shoot my ass.

We stay a few more hours talking and getting to know one another. We showed them the ultrasound pictures, and they promised to stop by one night this week to see where we live, where their daughter is now living.

Definitely lucky he didn't shoot my ass.

"That went well," Addyson says after we're home and getting ready for bed.

"He should have shot me," I tell her my earlier thoughts.

"What?" She laughs.

"If our daughter does what we did tonight, I don't know that I'll handle it that well."

"They just want to see me happy. You'll be the same way," she assures me.

"What are you doing?" I ask when I see her wheel out her small suitcase. I wheeled them both into the closet last night.

"Unpacking."

"Okay." I sit up on the bed, ready to help her if she needs it. "Want me to get the other one? You shouldn't be lifting."

"No, not tonight. Everything I need is in this one. And for the record, it only has a few things so it's not heavy."

I watch closely as she unzips the suitcase and pulls out her cowboy boots. She gives me a goofy grin, then turns and places them on the shoe rack in her closet. Yes, I thought ahead to give my future wife her own closet space. Addy says it was genius, so I'm good to go.

"No going back now," I tell her.

"Nope." She goes back to the suitcase and unwraps something that's in a towel. She walks to the dresser at the foot of the bed and places it on the corner.

When she steps back, I see it's a framed ultrasound picture. My heart flips over in my chest. This is really happening. The love of my life is here with me, living with me. We're having a baby and she's agreed to be my wife. A lot has happened in a very short amount of time, but I wouldn't change anything. Not any of it.

Unable to resist, I stand from the bed and make my way to the dresser. I trace the outline of the white frame that has *Baby* spelled out in block letters at the bottom. Pulling my eyes from my unborn child, I turn and see Addy place two more frames on the nightstand, by her side of the bed. The same two frames that sat beside her bed at her condo.

"There." She turns to face me with a smile.

In a few long strides, I'm standing before her. Leaning in, I bury my face in her neck, wrapping my arms around her. "That's all it takes," I tell her.

"What?" she asks when I pull back to look into those big brown eyes of hers.

"To make this house a home. All it took was you."

"Hmmm, maybe but I have my own theory on that one."

"Yeah? You care to enlighten me?"

"We're the difference," she says, a slow smile tilting her lips.

I kiss her. My lips on hers. Slowly, I slide my tongue past her lips, tasting and exploring her mouth. I'll never get enough of her.

Never.

"I missed you," I say against her lips.

She nods. "Show me." She raises her hands in the air. My hands move to the hem of her shirt pulling it up and over her head, tossing it on the floor. I step around her and gather her hair in my hand, moving it to lay over her shoulder. My lips press to the opposite bare shoulder as I free the clasp on her bra. She slides it down her shoulders and lets it fall from her grasp.

She turns to face me. "You're wearing too many clothes, Luke."

Mimicking her, I lift my hands in the air, bending down to her level and she rids me of my shirt. She unbuttons her shorts, pulling them and her panties to her ankles and stepping out. I do the same, kicking them off, not caring where they land. "You're breathtaking."

Stepping around me, she goes to the light switch by the door and kills the lights. I track her movement in the moonlight. When she reaches the bed, she pulls the covers back and climbs into bed. She rolls over facing the wall, and I climb in after her. I pull her into my arms, my cock nestled against her ass. Her soft skin under my fingertips.

"Luke," she whispers into the darkness of our room. "I just really need you to hold me. I need your arms around me, but I need you inside of me too. I need to feel you surround me."

I slide my leg between hers. My fingers find her center, and she's ready for me just like I knew she would be. Gripping my cock, I stroke once, then twice, coating myself with her before aligning myself with her entrance and pushing inside. She arches her back and I slide in deeper. My arms circle around her, holding her to me. "Like this?"

"Yes."

We're both quiet and still. Unmoving, I let her body pulse around me, proving yet again we were made for each other. One arm under her head, she uses me as a pillow. The one that surrounds her, palms her breast, scraping the pad of my thumb over her hard nipple.

"Luke," she breathes.

My hands trace over her chest down to her belly. "We made a baby, Addy." There's wonder in my voice. I never gave much thought to having kids, except for one day I would. Now that it's here, now I know that this beautiful woman in my arms is carrying our baby, I want a house full. I want this house bursting at the seams with our children. Their laughter and most of all, the love.

My hand slides further to find her clit. Slowly, my thumb traces in small circles. I'm ready, so I need her to be. Never in a million years would I say that just sliding inside of a woman could get me off, but then again, I'd never met Addy. Thinking about our life together and the life growing inside of her, the feel of her hot wet heat pulsing around me, it's enough.

She's enough.

Our bodies are so close, I can feel her breathing accelerate. "I love you," I whisper, kissing her bare shoulder. Her hand reaches back and grips my thigh. "You ready, baby?" I whisper huskily.

"Y-yes," she pants.

Pulling out then pushing back in, I cause us both to moan. My thumb continues to strum her clit as I leisurely push in and out of her. Her walls tighten around me.

"L-Luke," she pants.

"Let me have it, Addy. Let go." My words push her over the edge. She moans a deep throaty moan and pulls me over the edge with her. We lie in the darkness catching our breath. I don't want to move, and she doesn't seem to want to either.

"Goodnight, Lucas," she says over a yawn.

"Goodnight, beautiful," I whisper, closing my eyes. My arms are locked around her, and my cock that's still half-mast inside of her. Sleep claims me, and as I drift off, I'm more content than I've ever been in my life.

chapter
twenty-seven

Addyson

"You doing okay over there?" I ask Luke.

We're sitting in the exam room of my OBGYN waiting for the doctor to come in. It's my first appointment since I found out we were pregnant. Yes, we. Luke has made it a point to tell me that just because he can't carry the baby, he's still in this with me 100 percent. He's that guy. The one you know when he tells you that he loves you that it's unconditional. He's the one who runs out at midnight if you mention something sounds good. No joke. A couple of nights ago we were watching TV in bed, and I mentioned I'd like to have some Cheez-Its when I saw a commercial. He was out of bed, dressed, and out the door before I could protest. He was back fifteen minutes later with four tiny boxes from the twenty-four-hour gas station not far from our house.

"I'm good," he assures me with one of his smiles. It's one that has panties dropping everywhere. Lucky for me, it's also the smile he reserves just for me.

When the door opens, he sits up straighter in his chair. "Addyson," Dr. Edwards greets me. "How are you feeling?"

"Good, this is my fiancé, Lucas."

"Congratulations," Dr. Edwards says, shaking his hand. "How's Mom? Morning sickness? Cramping? All of which are normal," she adds.

"No to morning sickness. Some minimal cramping but nothing I can't handle."

"Good, that's your body making room for the little one." She goes on to talk about what's changing with the baby since my last visit and what will happen between now and our next one. "Right now your baby is about the size of a raspberry."

"So tiny," Lucas comments.

"Tiny, but mighty," she jokes. "How about we see if we can hear the heartbeat?"

Luke stands and walks to me. "Will that hurt either one of them?" he asks, concerned.

"Not at all. We use a doppler. It's external and completely safe."

His grip on my hand is firm as we watch Dr. Edwards place a wand on my still flat belly and move it around. Seconds tick by that feel like minutes. *Is something wrong? Why can't she find it?* There are a thousand questions running through my mind when I hear a steady thunderous beat fill the room.

"Nice and strong." Dr. Edwards smiles.

I hear Luke take a deep breath, and as if I needed that to remind me, I do the same. "Is it supposed to be that fast?" I ask her.

"Yes. Perfectly normal." She holds the wand still, letting us listen to our baby. "Everything looks great. We'll see you back at twelve weeks. Continue to take your prenatal vitamins, and if you need us before then, please don't hesitate to give us a call." She gathers the doppler, hands me a few paper towels to wipe the gel from my belly, and leaves the room.

"I love you." Lucas bends down and places a feather-soft kiss to my lips.

"I love you too." I smile up at him. "Can we go eat now or do you have to go back to work?"

"We can eat. I'm off the rest of the afternoon."

"Taco Bell?" I ask hopefully.

He laughs. "Anything you want, Addy."

After I climb off the exam table with his help, I get dressed. We stop at the desk and make my next appointment. Lucas puts it in his phone, and my heart stutters in my chest. How could I have ever believed he would hurt me? He loves with all that he is. I don't know what brought him to the bar that night, but I will be forever grateful he was there and interrupted our conversation.

As soon as we're in his truck, my phone rings. I smile when I see Harper's name. "Hello."

"Well, how did it go?" I hear the excitement in her voice.

"Everything looks good. We go back in four weeks."

"Come over to our place. We're throwing some burgers on the grill."

"Are you home?"

"Yeah, I called Just, and we wanted to celebrate with you and Luke, so we ended our days early. It's all set up."

I glance over at Luke. "Your choice, baby."

"Okay. We're headed there now. What can we bring? We can stop and get something."

"Nothing. Just your appetite. I'm so happy for you, Addyson. You deserve this happiness."

"So do you. See you soon," I tell her. "So…" I turn to Luke. "Taco Bell will just have to wait."

"We can go through the drive-thru and take it with us," he offers.

"No, that's fine. It just sounded good."

"You sure?"

"Positive. Besides, the chance to catch up with Harper is way more appealing. I've only seen her a few times in the last couple of weeks."

"That's because you were both busy moving to new places."

"I know. There have been so many changes, I don't want to lose my close friendship with her."

"You won't," he assures me.

When we get to Justin and Harper's, she rushes outside and pulls me into a hug. "I miss you, momma," she says, placing her hand on my belly.

"Is this how this pregnancy is going to go? You plan on feeling me up every time you see me?" I joke.

"Maybe. I can't wait until you start showing." She steps back and motions for us to follow her inside.

"Hey," Justin greets as we enter the living room. "How did the appointment go?"

"We heard the baby's heartbeat," Luke tells them. "It's this loud, fast whooshing sound. I can't explain it, but it was unreal."

"Congrats, man." Justin nods in our direction.

"Oh, I have something for you." Harper hops off the arm of the couch where Justin is sitting and grabs a small green bag before handing it to us.

"Harper, you didn't have to," I tell her.

"Hush. I'm Auntie Harper. I can buy my niece or nephew whatever I want."

I shake my head at her and begin pulling out the tissue paper. I throw my head back and laugh when I see what it is. "Really, Harp?"

"It's cute, right?"

I hold up the little yellow onesie to show Luke. *My aunt rocks!* is plastered on the front.

"Thanks." Luke smiles over at her.

She grins at us both. "I can't wait to throw you a shower. Have you thought about the room?" she asks.

"A little. But it's still early," I remind her. She knows I'm worried I could miscarry. The earliest chances are before twelve weeks. Luke and I agreed to not do anything to the house until we pass that mark.

"It's going to be fine," she assures me.

"Is this what we have to look forward to?" Justin asks Harper.

"Yes," she says softly. "Okay." She turns to look at us. "You ready to eat?"

"Yes," I say immediately, and they all laugh. "I'll help." I stand up and follow her to the kitchen. A few minutes later, the guys join us.

"I'll start the burgers." Justin kisses Harper on the lips, then takes the plate of hamburger patties from her.

She watches the guys step out on the deck, before turning back to me. "So mac and cheese with Velveeta. I know it's your fave."

"I love you."

She chuckles. "I love you too, Addy, and I'm so happy for you."

"I think this is going to be your future soon," I tell her.

"Maybe, if it is, I'll accept it with open arms. If not, I'm in no rush. I love him. I know we'll get there."

We get busy making the macaroni and cheese and catching up. Luke sticks his head in through the open door and tells us the burgers are ready and wants to know where we want to eat.

"Inside," Harper and I say at the same time. Luke just smiles and shakes his head.

We pile our plates with food and gather around the kitchen island. Harper and I talk about her plans to do some remodeling on the hotel she manages. Luke and Justin are talking shop as well. It's a great day with even better company.

"I'm stuffed." Harper stands.

"Harp, sit down. I'll get it."

"I've got it," she tells Justin.

"Babe, please," he says, and as if his words melt her, she slides back to her seat. When Justin stands and drops to one knee, I gasp and cover my mouth, not wanting to ruin the moment. "Harper Scott, I love you more today than yesterday, and I already know I'll love you even more tomorrow." He reaches into his pocket and pulls out a little black box. "Will you marry me?"

"Yes!" she screeches, pulling him to his feet and wrapping herself around him. Her hand shakes as he slides the ring on her finger.

We congratulate them with a round of hugs, and Harper and I make plans to have dinner this week to start planning our weddings. Lucas and I thank them for dinner before heading home.

"We couldn't have asked for a better day," Lucas says, pulling his shirt over his head.

"I agree. I'm so happy for them." I say where I'm lounging on our bed.

Lucas climbs on the bed beside me and slides his arm under my head. He snuggles in close, resting his hand on my belly. My sweater is short and has ridden up a little. The feel of his skin against mine is something I cherish. I turn into him and run my fingers over his short beard.

"More than just that. I'm still in awe of hearing our baby's heartbeat. It's a miracle that this tiny human the size of a raspberry is growing inside of you." He rests his forehead against mine.

"It's surreal," I agree.

He closes his eyes, but I keep mine open, watching him. "I promise you and this baby I'll always be there. I'll love you both with everything in me. I know that all of this is fast, Addy, but that doesn't make it any less real. I want you. I want this baby, and I want this life we're building together. I want more babies," he says softly. "But most of all, I want to always be the difference for you. I want to be the one you know you can count on no matter what the situation or the outcome. Through good times and in bad, I want you always."

"Sounds like you just wrote your vows," I say softly.

"Speaking of vows." He opens his eyes. "You ready to start planning our wedding?"

"I already have."

He props himself up on his elbows. "Really?"

"Yes. I want to have it here. Just our immediate friends and family. Small and intimate. Our love is big. We don't need all the pomp and ceremony. I just want to marry you."

"Anything you want."

"What about you? Did you want a big wedding?"

"Does any guy want a big wedding?" A smile stretches his lips, making my heart flip with happiness. "All that matters at the end of the day is you becoming Addyson Grace Prescott." He kisses my nose. "When?"

"Soon. I'd like to not be showing, or barely showing."

"Done. You tell me when and what I need to do, and it's done. I don't know the first thing about planning a wedding, but I can follow directions."

"I don't want it to be stressful. I want to keep it simple."

"How about we plan a get-together, tell our friends and family it's just to get everyone together. When they get here, it's our wedding?" he asks, excitement in his voice.

"I love it. No fanfare, just us and those we value the most."

"I love you, Addy."

"I love you too, Luke."

epilogue
* * * *

Four Years Later...

LUCAS

I stand off to the side of the room watching my wife. She's sitting on the couch, our three-and-a-half-year-old daughter, Emma Grace, on her lap, and our one-month-old son, Graham Lucas, on Emma's lap. Addy has the patience of a saint when it comes to our children. Hell, with life. Nothing seems to faze her. Earlier today, Emma came into the living room with a poopy diaper hanging from her hands. She was so proud of herself that she changed her baby's diaper. Addy rushed out of the room to check on Graham who was sleeping peacefully in the bassinet beside our bed.

I was still standing there, with a shitty diaper in my hands, looking down at my daughter who is the spitting image of her mamma. I was getting ready to scold her, which only makes us both feel like shit. When those big brown eyes, that are so much Addyson, well with tears, I'm a goner. The problem with that is my Emma knows my weakness. Before I could get on her,

Addyson was back in the living room kneeling before her. That's when the truth came out.

Emma took a dirty diaper from the diaper pail and put it on her baby, the one Addy found in the hallway, with shit all over it. They tell you parenting is a challenge, but they don't mention all the bodily functions that happen. For instance, my son used to piss on me every single time I changed his diaper. Finally, Addyson took pity on me and showed me how to maneuver to cover him up with the new diaper so I miss the spray. Like I said, my wife has the patience of a saint. She is the backbone of our family.

Today, our parents, as well as Harper and Justin are here to welcome baby Graham home. We did the same thing with Emma. Once we get settled, we invite them all over for some food and family time.

"Daddy!" Siler, my two-year-old son says, rushing toward me. He wraps his little arms around my legs squeezing as tight as he can. "Up." He holds out his arms for me to lift him.

"What's up?" I ask him.

"Take the baby." He points to the couch.

"That's your baby brother. We love him," I tell him. He's not taking too kindly to no longer being the baby in the family.

"My mommy."

"She is your mommy, but she's Graham's mommy too, and Emma's."

"Siler," my dad says, joining us. "You know you have to teach Graham how to play when he gets older. He's going to need his big brother to show him the ropes."

"Take baby," he says.

"Nice try, Dad. He's two," I remind him.

"Come to Gramps. We'll go outside and throw the ball."

"Ball!" Siler cheers, and leaps from my arms to Dad's. Mom meets them at the door and they disappear outside.

I watch as my mother-in-law steals Graham from Addy, while my father-in-law holds his hand out for Emma. She skips off with him as they head outside as well. Harper and Justin are already in the pool with their two-and-a-half-year-old, Sadie. She just told us earlier today that they're expecting baby number two. I enjoy giving Justin a hard time telling him he needs to catch up. They had trouble conceiving at first, but this time around things seemed to happen faster for them. I'm glad. They deserve it.

"What are you doing over here?" Addy asks, snaking her arms around my waist.

"Just thinking."

"Oh, yeah? About what?" She looks up at me, and to this day, I still see nothing but love shining back at me.

"About us, life, our family. How that night I walked into Stagger I didn't realize what my life was missing. Not until I walked past your table and decided to butt into your conversation."

"Never in a million years did I see this becoming our lives."

"You happy?" I ask her this question a lot because if the answer is ever no, I have work to do whatever it takes to make her happy. She's given me so much. However, she always says the same thing.

"Deliriously happy."

I pull her into me and place a kiss on her temple. "Love you," I whisper.

"I love you too." She places her hands on either side of my face. "How could I not? You're the difference."

contact
kaylee ryan

I cannot thank you enough for taking the time to read The Difference.
I'd love to hear from you.

Facebook: http://bit.ly/2C5DgdF

Reader Group: http://bit.ly/2O0yWDx

Goodreads: http://bit.ly/2HodJvx

BookBub: http://bit.ly/2KulVvH

Website: www.kayleeryan.com/

also by
kaylee ryan

acknowledgments

* * * *

To my readers:

Twenty-five books! When I published my first book almost six years ago, I never could have imaged that this is where I would be. I cannot tell you how much it means to me to have you on this ride with me. You're making my dreams a reality. Sure, it takes hard work, a great team and a lot of dedication on my end, but to know you're all out there reading my words, and falling in love with my characters as I do. That's humbling beyond belief. Thank you so much for taking a chance on me.

To my family:

I love you. You hold me up and support me every day. I can't imagine my life without you as my support system. Thank you for believing in me, and being there to celebrate my success.

Sara Eirew:

Thank you for another cover worthy image.

Tami Integrity Formatting:

Thank you for making The Difference paperback beautiful. You're amazing and I cannot thank you enough for all that you do.

Sommer Stein:

Time and time again, you wow me with your talent. Thank you for another amazing cover.

My beta team:

Jamie, Stacy, Lauren, and Franci I would be lost without you. You read my words as much as I do, and I can't tell you what your input and all the time you give means to me. Countless messages and bouncing idea, you ladies keep me sane with the characters are being anything but. Thank you from the bottom of my heart for taking this wild ride with me.

Give Me Books:

With every release, your team works diligently to get my book in the hands of bloggers. I cannot tell you how thankful I am for your services.

Tempting Illustrations:

Thank you for everything. I would be lost without you.

Julie Deaton:

Thank you for giving this book a set of fresh final eyes.

Becky Johnson:

I could not do this without you. Thank you for pushing me, and making me work for it.

Marisa Corvisiero:

Thank you for all that you do. I know I'm not the easiest client. I'm blessed to have you on this journey with me.

Kimberly Ann:

Thank you for organizing and tracking the ARC team. I couldn't do it without you.

Bloggers:

Thank you, doesn't seem like enough. You don't get paid to do what you do. It's from the kindness of your heart and your love of reading that fuels you. Without you, without your pages, your voice, your reviews, spreading the word it would be so much harder if not impossible to get my words in reader's hands. I can't tell you how much your never-ending support means to me. Thank you for being you, thank you for all that you do.

To my Kick Ass Crew:

The name of the group speaks for itself. You ladies truly do KICK ASS! I'm honored to have you on this journey with me. Thank you for reading, sharing, commenting, suggesting, the teasers, the messages all of it. Thank you from the bottom of my heart for all that you do. Your support is everything!

With Love,

Kaylee Ryan
AUTHOR

CPSIA information can be obtained
at www.ICGtesting.com
Printed in the USA
FSHW010713020619
58653FS